WILLOW

A Promised Land Romance

WILLOW

•

Carolyn Brown

AVALON BOOKS
NEW YORK

PRINTED IN THE UNITED STATES OF AMERICA
ON ACID-FREE PAPER
BY HADDON CRAFTSMEN, BLOOMSBURG, PENNSYLVANIA

To my only sister . . . Patricia Gail Gray Russell.
Fate made us sisters. Hearts made us best friends.

ACKNOWLEDGMENTS

My gratitude and appreciation to everyone who continues to read my books. As I've said so many times, without readers, writers would quickly find themselves on the endangered species list. So Doris, Barbara, Alesha, Selma, Debbie, Tammy Buckaloo, Maxine, Fada, Retha, Linda, Gloria, Betty. Lawana, Juanita, jhale, Sonya, Jana, Willie, Audrey, Sue, Sharon, Karynn, Yvonne, Janelle, Helen, Mary, Maxine, Phyllis, Sissy, Randi, Jessie, Lanelle, Susan, Marlene, Lori and Cindy and the many, many other friends, kith and kin who call, e-mail, write or stop me on the street to offer encouragement, I thank you. You are truly the wind beneath my wings.

Chapter One

Willow brushed the dust from her dark blue traveling skirt and tucked an errant wisp of curly blond hair back into the bun at the nape of her long, aristocratic neck. Twenty-five days she'd spent in a series of uncomfortable stagecoaches—after the first ten she'd begun to have serious doubts about the whole trip. Jake Dulan had certainly made no effort to even show his face one time in Mercersberg, Pennsylvania all these years, so why in the devil was she putting herself through almost four weeks of sheer misery just to lay eyes on the man before he bit the dust?

The stagecoach came to an abrupt halt, sending her sliding across the seat. Willow was thankful the obese man she'd shared the coach with the day before had gotten off at the previous stop. Her nostrils flared at the very idea of touching the smelly fellow. The door opened and she brushed the driver's hand away and stepped out into the bright spring morning without any help. She might look like a simpering belle who couldn't even crawl out of a coach by herself, but looks were deceiving. She could very well get out of a coach unassisted.

After long, boring days of riding in something akin to a boat on dry land, with all its bouncing around, she'd finally arrived in St. Joseph, Missouri. And it wasn't one blessed

1

thing like she'd pictured in her mind when she left Mercersberg. Willow gasped just slightly when she looked up at the four-story brick hotel standing like a fortress in front of her. She'd assumed the hotel where Jake made reservations for her would be at best a two-story shack in dire need of paint, with saggy mattresses and creaky wooden stairs that hadn't been dusted since the great flood. But not so. The Patee House came close to intimidating Willow, and nothing had intimidated her since she was five years old and went to live with Great-Aunt Harriet.

"Not what you were expecting?" The coach driver spit a stream of brown tobacco onto the green lawn. "They tell me there's a hundred and forty rooms in that place. Full this time of year with folks waiting for the wagon trains to take them west to the promised land. Fools. That's what they all are. There ain't no promised land."

Young men in dark trousers and white shirts with boiled collars emerged from the front doors and carried the passenger's luggage inside. Willow watched her rolltop steamer trunk carefully. It contained every single thing she owned and there was no going back. Not now. She'd been told if she made the decision to walk out the door to go see low-life Jake Dulan, she wasn't ever to let her shadow fall across the threshold again. Those were Uncle Herman and Aunt Nellie's final words on the issue. The fight she'd had with Pete Hanson just moments before she left wouldn't bear repeating even in the confines of her mind. Yes, she'd cut all ties in hopes of settling the questions lying unanswered in her heart.

"Well, at least Jake Dulan has good taste and evidently lots of money," she mumbled as she made her way to the registration desk. A young man wearing crisply creased dark trousers and a white shirt with a black garter around his bicep looked up with a question in his eyes.

"I'm Willow Dulan. Reservations have been made for me," she said, looking forward to a long, hot bath before meeting with Jake. What would he look like? Talk like?

Would he tell her why he'd disappeared without ever even trying to locate her before now?

"Ah, yes, we've been expecting you for days," he nodded. "But I am afraid, my dear lady, there is bad news awaiting your journey's end. Jake Dulan died day before yesterday. They are at this moment, even as we speak, having his funeral."

Willow's heart sank. A trip from the depths of Hades, questions upon questions, and all for naught. "Where?" she asked.

"Why, down at the white church. I'll call a driver and buggy for you." He snapped his fingers and a young boy came running. "Miss Willow here needs to be at the church where they are having the funeral for Jake Dulan. Take her and make haste. She's already missed the first hymn, I'm sure. Your trunk will be taken to your room, ma'am. Do you require a lady to unpack it for you?"

"It's locked and no, I do not want anyone to unpack it for me." She followed the boy outside.

Willow sighed as she climbed into the buggy. Drat Jake's sorry hide forevermore. He could have hung on another day or two so she could have at least seen him alive. "How far is the church?" she asked the driver.

"Not far. Just down at the end of the street. Little white church. Hank and the boys is already there with the others. You'll just miss the first of the preachin'," the young man said. "That Jake Dulan was a man's man. I really liked him. Met him last year when I went to work at the Patee House. Good man, that Jake was. Sorry you done almost missed the funeral, ma'am."

Willow didn't answer. What could she say? That she didn't even want to go to the funeral? That evidently the fellow driving the buggy knew more about Jake than she did? She hadn't come halfway across the continent to look at a corpse in a wooden box. She'd come for answers and to set the restlessness in her heart aright. When the buggy stopped, she straightened her bonnet, stiffened her back, let the young man help her out of the buggy, and tip-toed up on the porch. She wanted to stomp up those four steps so badly that she had to clamp her jaw in determination to keep from giving in to the urge. Aunt Harriet would rise up from her grave if she was anything less than a lady at a funeral. No matter who'd died.

She slung open the doors of the church and stopped for a moment in the vestibule. The preacher was droning on in a monotone about the late, great Jake Dulan. How he'd taken many, many poor souls across the continent to their own promised land called California. And now he'd come to his end and was in the real promised land, where sorrow and pain were no more.

One man sat on the back row and four women were scattered in the other pews. Not many mourners for a dead man, but then Jake probably didn't leave many friends. Not if even one word her aunt said about him was true. Matter of fact, if what Aunt Harriet said was true, it was a wonder that the preacher wasn't delivering his sermon to an empty church.

One thing for absolutely sure, Willow wouldn't need to pull the hanky from the sleeve of her jacket. Of all the blasted luck, anyway. Nineteen years old and not even a deathbed confession as to why Jake had left her and her mother to fend for themselves all those years ago. Dead. Jake Dulan was dead. After endless days of riding in a stage-coach from Mercersberg, Pennsylvania to St. Joe, Missouri. Staying in dark dingy rooms. Eating horrid food. Sharing space with smelly men, bored children, and travel-tired, sharp-tongued women. All for nothing but a funeral. She still wouldn't have any answers. Not a single one. If Jake Dulan hadn't already stopped breathing, she would have gladly taken the little pistol from the velvet drawstring ret-icule she carried over her arm and shot him a few inches to the left of dead center of the third button on his shirt.

She slid into a pew toward the back of the church and attempted to listen to what the preacher said. Maybe he'd known Jake and at least she'd hear a few words about the man who'd fathered her. But her attention was quickly drawn from the silky smooth monotonous voice of the preacher to the other people in the church. Who were those other four women anyway? Evidently, Jake had been some kind of wagon train master, from what the preacher said, so that would explain the man sitting on the front pew. Maybe the women were his aunts? His sisters? Or cousins? She pondered over the idea for a few minutes then decided it really didn't matter. She went back to listening to the preacher drone on and on about the "dearly departed." She wanted to march up the center aisle, slap him silly, push him away from the podium, and tell the people there just what a sorry skunk Jake Dulan really was.

If all a body had to do to gain entrance through the pearly gates was stop breathing then Jake Dulan was sitting on a big fluffy cloud visiting with St. Peter. If it took any more than that, then he was probably sitting on a barbed wire fence in hell's back forty acres informing Lucifer about the changes he intended to make.

Jake wasn't a saint while he lived, but the preacher sure made him sound like one as he ran down the list of the man's sparkling qualities. Sitting on the back pew of the church, watching five very different women arrive one at a time, Hank realized the preacher knew absolutely nothing about his wagon train partner. Hank figured he could have given Jake a much more proper sendoff. He would have just propped him up against the bar over at the hotel, pressed his cold, stiff fingers around a double shot of the meanest whiskey the bartender could pour, and sat there beside him listening to the piano player pound on the keys. Now that's the way old Jake should've been put to rest, not laid out like some Sunday school teacher in a black suit and tie.

However, that's what Jake wanted. A fine sendoff for the girls. As much as it went against Hank's grain, he'd fixed

it all up proper. Just like Jake had said to do. Even paid
the preacher to stand up there and go on for at least forty-
five minutes. All for those five women, who were the only
other people in the whole church, other than Hank and the
crew, who were acting as pallbearers. He was just glad the
last of the women made it on time to see Jake put away
proper. Hank hadn't expected a full house. Not in a church.
Now if it had been over at Sterling's Silver Palace there
would have been a different tale to tell. Every one of the
boys would have been raising a shot glass filled to the brim
in a toast to all the good times they'd shared with Jake.

The preacher finally said a brief prayer. The final "amen"
was stilling hanging in the cool spring morning when two
ladies stepped in from a side room, opened their song
books, and sang a mournful hymn. Now, that had cost more
than Jake had put by for such a thing, but he'd been pretty
definite in his wishes, so Hank had coughed up the rest of
the money. Now he was sorry he'd done it. Not one of the
five women was shedding a single tear. They were all sitting with backs ramrod straight and heads high. Not a sob
amongst them. The funeral wasn't going like Jake wanted
it to at all. They were supposed to be weeping in their little
lace hankies by now. Lord, it's a wonder Jake Dulan's spirit
didn't bust the nails right out of the top of that coffin and
raise up from the dead. Spending so much on a proper
funeral so those five women could have one good last memory, and not a one of them appreciating it like they should.

When the last note died deader than old Jake Dulan, six
of Hank's hired hands took their places in front of the casket. Every one of them looked like they'd much rather be
pinching the white tops off chicken manure than standing
there in a church fixing to carry Jake's casket to the cemetery. But they'd do what Hank and Jake asked of them,
even if it did go against their grain to see those five women
acting so uppity. Too bad. Old Jake would be disappointed
that not a one of them had wept over his lifeless remains.

"And now, dear friends, these fine young men will carry

our dearly departed brother, Jake Dulan, to his final resting place in the church cemetery right next to the building here. If you will follow behind me, we will make a procession to the grave site."

"Dust to dust and ashes to ashes." The preacher recited from a little black book he held in his chubby hands as the wooden casket was lowered into the six-foot hole by a half dozen strong men.

Willow wondered if the other women would introduce themselves to her. Or if the fellow with the worn and tattered hat in his hands might at least say something. Her stomach growled, reminding her she hadn't eaten since the night before. She'd overslept that morning and had barely made it to the stage in time to get her trunk loaded. Seemed a shame to be standing there among all those strangers and one dead father while starving to death.

"May the soul of Jake Dulan rest in peace," the preacher said. "I will leave you fine people to your mourning now. The undertaker will cover the grave when you are finished with your last moments here."

Hank nodded. The next part wasn't going to be a bit easier than this had been. The time had come when he had to listen to Jake's last will and testament as it was being read to the five women. He already knew what was in it and had tried his danged level best to keep Jake from writing it up that way, but Jake had his own views and declared that was just the way he wanted it put down.

Heaven help Hank after it was read. There'd be a catfight for sure. He just hoped he'd be out of the room before it began. Thank goodness he'd be leaving St. Joseph in a couple of days. He just needed a few more women to sign on to his wagon train and then he would set out for California, to a little town named Bryte where many men waited for brides. It would be Hank's last trip. If he survived it, he would have well earned the double pay they'd given him for the job. Even as tough as he was, he sure enough didn't look forward to more than a hundred whining women for the better part of nine months.

Nine months. Strange, that's how long it took to make a baby. By the time he reached Bryte he would probably feel like he'd given birth. He smiled at that idea and looked up to see five sets of blue eyes staring right at him. Every single one of them had Jake Dulan's eyes. The rest of them were as different as their mothers had been, but Jake couldn't have denied a one of them. Not with those strange aqua-colored eyes.

"My name is Hank Gibson. I was Jake Dulan's friend and business partner. In the past seventeen years we've brought so many wagon trains across this land, I've lost count of them. Must be at least sixteen, or maybe even more 'cause a couple of them didn't go all the way to the coast. I'm glad you could all come to the funeral. It would've meant a lot to him. Glad you got here on time, too. Could we go to the hotel? I've reserved a private dining room so we can continue this business there," Hank said.

Willow and the other women followed wordlessly to a black buggy waiting at the edge of the cemetery lawn. All but one pallbearer disappeared down the street to a saloon, where the tinkly sound of piano music drifted out with the deep laughter of men and the high-pitched giggles of women. The remaining fellow, a tall, handsome man with dark hair curling on his shirt collar and the softest brown eyes Willow had ever seen, rode his horse behind the buggy carrying them back to the hotel.

The room Hank led them to took Willow's breath away. Honey-colored brocaded silk covered the walls. Light sparkled from the glow of candles set in a crystal chandelier. Not even the Sudderfields of Mercersberg, with their airs and three-story mansion, could have walked into that room and not stared like country bumpkins. Willow mustered up a healthy dose of bluff to go with her spitfire courage and let a waiter seat her at the long, shiny mahogany table with matching cushy chairs. No one needed to know that she felt a little green around the mouth and more than a little jittery.

Hank ordered two pitchers of lemonade. The waitress poured seven glasses and flirted with the handsome pall-bearer the whole time. Willow had the strangest desire to dump the sticky sweet liquid right down the front of her low-cut dress. Her decision to come to Missouri had come at great cost. She'd cut all ties with her family and now she was in a strange place that scared the devil out of her. Not even the biggest hotel in Mercersberg could compare to this and she'd thought she was coming out to some kind of wilderness. When she got the traveling ticket, the money for food on the journey, and the hotel reservation letter, she'd never figured on arriving too late to even talk to her father. And she'd sure never thought about staying in a hotel like the Patee House. The silly waitress could do her job and get on out of the room so they could hear what the wagon master had to say. Aggravation was what she felt. Along with agitation, irritation, and a healthy dose of pure old mad. All because Jake Dulan had the indecency to die before she could get there.

Hank got to his feet. "Now, I've got Jake's last will and testament. He wanted me to read it to you all together right after the funeral. Rafe here is going to read it to you. I can make out a few words but I'm not the reader Rafe is or the writer that Jake was. Jake was my partner and my friend and I'm glad to fix things up the way he wanted. It would make him proud to know that you were finally all together in one place, even if it was at his funeral. Now Rafe, you break the seal on that letter and commence to reading," Hank said.

"Okay," Rafe said in a deep resonant voice. "It says:

If Rafe or Hank is making out these words then it means I'm dead. I guess I waited too long to send for you because if I would've been alive I would have

maybe made some revisions on this letter. But prob-
ably not, now that I give it some thought. I didn't
change anything concerning you five before so why
would I change it now? So I'll just get on with the
story. I am dying with the consumption. Can't even
enjoy my cigars and whiskey anymore and I won't be
making this last trip to California with Hank and the
boys. So I'm going to put down a few things here and
now. To get on with the story, this is the way it is.
When I was a young man, like all young men, I fell
in love. She was a little wisp of a lady with gorgeous
red hair.

Rafe stopped for a minute and looked up. Surely he was
talking about the mother of the girl with the thick auburn
hair.

"Momma didn't have red hair," Willow said. "She was
a blond, just like me."

"No talking until the letter is finished," Hank declared.
"That's the way Jake wanted it. Just for you all to sit right
here and listen. You can talk all you want when Rafe is
done."

We were so much in love, Rafe went on.

We bought a little farm in Tennessee and life was go-
ing to be wonderful. We were going to have a house
full of sons. The first one was going to be named Jacob
Edward Dulan, Junior. Only the first one wasn't a
boy. It was a girl and my wife died in childbirth. I
named the child Augusta after my mother, gave her
and my farm to my wife's parents, and left. I didn't
want a daughter to remind me of my wife every day.
I wanted a son.

The tallest of the five women looked up with a chill in
her light blue eyes. "I'm Augusta. Only they call me Gussie," she said in a soft Southern voice.

Willow's heart skipped a beat. She stared rudely at Augusta . . . Gussie. A sister. Lord have mercy, she'd never figured on finding a sister at the funeral. Somehow, she'd always thought she was the only child Jake Dulan ever produced. Neither Great-Aunt Harriet nor Aunt Nellie ever mentioned Jake having another child. Evidently there were things about Jake that even Helen, Willow's mother, didn't know.

Rafe went on.

If you're sitting in the room right now, Augusta Dulan, rest assured I didn't hate you. After all, you were my flesh and blood, but you were just a girl. My world didn't have room for daughters. I wanted a ranch and big strong sons to help me run it. Sons that would produce more sons and the Dulan name would go on and on throughout the history books. No, my child, I didn't hate you at all. I just didn't want to stick around Tennessee and raise up a girl child. I swore I'd never marry again, but I changed my mind a few months later over in Arkansas. She was another red-haired beauty. I thought I'd found the right woman to produce sons but I figured wrong. The baby was a girl— that'd be you, Garnet Diana. I was worried she'd die in the birthing but she lived and promised me the next one would be a big strapping boy. I decided I'd stay on in those mountains with her. She got bit by a rattlesnake while she was drawing water from the well when you was six weeks old. Died two days later. Figured it was a sure sign for me to be on my way. You were supposed to be a boy, after all, and it wasn't so hard to up and leave a screaming, red-haired girl baby behind. I'd already done it once. I left you with your grandparents and moved on to South Carolina.

Then I met a tall, brown-haired preacher's daughter. She just took my heart away and we was married about a month later. The third time is supposed to be the charm. It wasn't. She produced a girl for me that next spring. You, Velvet Jane. Even though you wasn't the son we wanted, and I had the itch to move on when you was born, I stayed around. I was tired of marryin' and buryin'. She promised she'd keep on having babies until I had a yard full of mean boys. She died of the fever when you was six months old. Seemed like an omen to me so I let your grandmother have you and I took off again.

Went to Texas and a little Mexican gal took a shine to me. I still had a hankering for sons and Maria promised to have me a bunch of brown-eyed, dark-haired boys. I figured maybe someday I'd send for you three girls to go with them. But I decided to wait and see what happened before I told Maria I already had three daughters strung out over three states. Lord, but that Maria had a temper. If she'd a'knowed about the first three, she'd a'been a pure pain to live with. I kept hoping that the baby would be a boy. It wasn't, though, and I guess I wasn't even surprised. We named you Gypsy Rose. The next year my Maria produced a big, beautiful son. She died doing it and the baby was stillborn.

Girls, girls, girls. Four of them by then, scattered from Tennessee to south Texas. All I wanted was a son but I was tired of burying wives so I really swore off marriage. At least until I went to Virginia and met up with a Southern belle named Helen. After a whirlwind of a courtship we was married. I'd lost all hope of a son by then and she didn't disappoint me. The screaming red-faced baby was still yet another girl. I didn't give a hoot what she named you, but she decided on Willow Gail. She didn't die when you was born and she didn't die a year later. I kept expecting her to drop down dead anytime but she didn't and after another year went by we found out we just flat didn't like each other. Only wife I'd had that I didn't love with my *whole heart and want to share sons with and she lived. One day I came home from the fields and she was packing. Said she'd had all she could stand of me and was going to Pennsylvania to live close to her brother and sister. Tell the truth, I was mighty glad to see her leave. I had the roaming itch again. But after five disappointments I just plumb given up on sons by then. I've been running wagon trains ever since with Hank.*

So that's the story, girls. You are gathered together to hear my will. It's this. I've spent every last cent I own to bring you together at my deathbed or my funeral. All I'm leaving you is each other. You are five sisters. Dulan blood. Mothers as different as night and day. But the same father. Get to know each other. You might find something you like. If there is you can rest assured it's my blood coming out because your mothers would have all hated each other.

Signed, Jake Dulan.

Rafe laid the letter in the middle of the table. Oppressive silence hung like a heavy fog among the women as they studied one face and then another. Sisters. Five of them. With a rascal like Jake for a father. If Willow had had to speak or die right then, she would have just had to think her final prayers. Of every scenario she'd imagined on the long trip, this had to take the cake.

"Which one of you is Willow? And do you really have a mother?" Gussie asked bluntly, the words cutting through the silence like the sound of a shot in a church house during prayers.

"I'm Willow, and my mother died of consumption when I was five years old," Willow answered just as sharply. None of them need look down on her. At least Jake admitted to loving their mothers. He just plain didn't like hers.

"Me and Rafe are going to leave you girls here now. We got to rustle up a few more women before our wagon train takes off to California in a few days," Hank explained, getting up so fast his chair fell over backwards.

"What?" Willow eyed the tall cowboy who'd read the letter. "What are you talking about? You're going to leave us here in this forsaken place with nothing?"

"Hey, Jake was my friend, but I didn't hire on this trip to take care of his daughters, lady," Rafe said. "All I said I'd do was read that letter. Now I've done it and we're going to attend to our business. We're takin' a train of new brides to California for a bunch of gold miners who hit it big and we ain't got time to be gee-hawing with you girls on what you intend to do now. That's your problem."

"You got rooms for one week," Hank said. "And your meals have been paid for during that week. After that, you're on your own."

"That low down skunk," Garnet hissed. "Well, girls, let's go up to my room and decide what we intend to do about this mess."

"Which one are you?" Willow asked.

"Garnet Diana Dulan. The one from Arkansas. Guess you are the youngest and come the fartherest to find there ain't nothing but a funeral. Well, honey, let me tell you I didn't leave nothing in Arkansas that I intend to go back and claim. Sounds like the best thing for us to do is at least get to know each other this week and decide just exactly what the devil we intend to do to keep our body and soul together when the room rent and meals play out."

"I guess so," Willow said, tossing back the rest of the lemonade as she stood up. "Sisters. Five of us. Lord have mercy!"

"Amen," the other four mouthed together at the same time.

Chapter Two

"What can I do for you ladies?" Hank looked up over the top of his gold-rimmed spectacles perched on the end of his crooked nose. That crazy sensation at the nape of his neck that always warned him there was trouble on the wind set up a prickling itch. He combed his graying hair with his fingertips and dug at the itching sensation with blunt fingernails.

"We're here to learn more about this wagon train deal you got going," Gussie said, holding up a flyer she'd picked up at the front desk. "Is it true there's men out there in California who's willing to pay our way to come out there and marry up with them?"

"It's true, but I just signed on my last lady, five minutes ago, so the bill has been filled. We'll leave day after tomorrow morning, bright and early. That's when the ferry can take us across the river. The supplies have been ordered for weeks, so now the wagons will be loaded. Surely you all weren't interested in this kind of thing?" he asked, amazed.

"We are," Willow said. "How many women you got?"

"I've got a hundred and two. I need a hundred so I've got two extras in case of emergencies. I've been on enough trips to know that we'll lose a couple. There's a hundred men waiting impatiently for brides at the end of the journey. And it's my last trip. I'm retiring to Nebraska when this is done. Got a spread waiting on me right beside Rafe's." He grinned.

"You are a fool." Garnet eyed Hank. "Let's go, girls. I wouldn't go with him even if he paid me big bucks and promised I wouldn't have to marry up with a man less'n I wanted to."

"Wait a minute." Hank stood up so fast several papers fell on the floor. "Who are you calling a fool?"

"You," Willow said bluntly. "And she's right. You need a hundred women. There's rattlesnakes and diseases out there, Hank. You're smart enough to know that not everyone on a wagon train makes it from start to finish. You're going to lose a few women, not just two. I'd be willing to lay odds that more than two will quit you before you get there. And you'll bury a couple on the way, too. What're you going to do when you get there and four or five men have to be told their money didn't bring them a wife? That they've waited a year for nothing? Then they got to stand around with their hands in their pockets while other men are happy as larks with their new women. How much money you going to refund to those four or five?"

"You're just full of information for someone who's never been on a wagon train before." Hank snorted. His neck itched so bad he had to fight his hands to keep from digging at it. At least his senses hadn't failed him. Trouble did come on the wind. Right into his rented office room in the form of five Dulan women.

"Tell you what," Gypsy said. "You sign us on and we'll make a deal with you. When you get there if you still got a hundred women then we'll step aside and let the first hundred women have the menfolks. We'll just be your insurance. How's that for a deal?"

Hank eyed them. *Lord have mercy, Jake's daughters on a wagon train.* His neck would itch the whole way to California. Neck, nothing! He'd be a solid case of hives by the time they reached their journey's end. They weren't wife material. At least not wife material in the wilds of California. They might survive in a fancy Eastern or Southern parlor, where they could sit in comfort while they entertained the ladies of the town. Not a one of them looked mean or tough enough to endure the first week of what lay in store for the women who'd put their name on the line, promising they'd show up for the beginning of the journey. No, he wouldn't be taking these frilly women with him. Besides, Jake had told Hank all about their mothers. Fine, educated lasses, but delicate as butterfly wings.

Even if they did have a few of Jake's traits, it just solidified his reserve in not taking them. If any one of them had inherited their father's tendency toward a hot temper with a short fuse, it could make for a lot of problems. Traveling with more than a hundred women was going to be enough of a job without five of Jake Dulan's offspring along for the ride. No, he wouldn't let them talk him into such a crazy notion. He had his built-in extra two women, and he was the wagon master, not five unruly women. He had twenty-two wagons; five or six women to each wagon and a couple of extra wagons to haul supplies.

"No." Hank shook his head firmly.

Rafe pushed open the door and stopped in his tracks when he saw the women surrounding Hank's desk. He raised a dark eyebrow at Hank, who looked like he could chew up wagon tongues and spit out round toothpicks. "You ladies want a copy of that last wil! or something?" he asked gruffly.

"No, they want to sign on to go to California," Hank said tersely.

A wide grin deepened the cleft in Rafe's chin when he chuckled. Now wasn't that the funniest thing he'd heard in months. Jake's spoiled rotten daughters on a wagon train for six to nine months. That little blond-haired one wouldn't last from dawn to dusk on the first day.

"What's so funny, cowboy?" Willow poked him in the

chest with her index finger. "Just what are you laughing at?"

"You, honey. I'm laughing at you more than any one of these other ones." Rafe slapped her hand away. "That's the funniest thing I've heard in months. You on a wagon train. Wouldn't be a solitary soul to button up your cute little boots every morning, or keep all the curls in that blond hair neither. This is for women who are tough enough to walk across half a continent to find a husband. And then work at being a wife and mother to his children. It's not a lark, honey. It's real business and you ain't the kind to hold up. I bet you ain't never even put those little white hands in a pan of dishwater, much less held the reins of a team of oxen."

Rafe Pierce had known women like Willow Dulan in his lifetime. Matter of fact he'd known one recently right up close and personal and there wasn't no way that cute little blond was going to California. Not if he had anything to say about it. Granted he was only working for a month, just until Tavish O'Leary could take over for him, but Rafe wasn't going to listen to this snit of a girl cry every time she broke a fingernail or sunburned her flawless skin.

"Well, who died and made you God?" Willow continued to punctuate each word with a poke in Rafe's chest.

"Not God, Willow. Rafe is a shortened form of Rafael, who was just an angel. Not God, Himself," Velvet said, having trouble keeping amusement from her voice. Lord, but she'd love to have the kind of nerve Willow had. Just to walk right up to a man who towered above her and jab him in the chest.

"Well, he don't look like no angel to me and I don't have to listen to what he's got to say. He's just the hired help and the decision is not his to make," Willow said.

Rafe blushed in spite of his resolve and anger.

"Is that true? Are you named for the angel who blows the trumpet?" Willow asked.

"No, Rafael was the angel who stirred up the waters of

the healing pool in the Bible. Don't you know your stories?" Velvet asked.

"I know that story but it sure don't say nothing about his name being Rafael," Willow said bluntly. "Aunt Harriet hauled me to church every Sunday morning and I've heard all the stories. But I'll believe you, Velvet." Willow's light eyes danced with anger as she glared back at Rafe. "You always judge the books by the covers? You don't know me, cowboy, so don't be so quick to judge."

"Oh, yeah?" Rafe said, drawing himself all the way to the top of his six-foot height to intimidate her. "I know your kind. You think you'll walk along and pick wildflowers, and demand the whole train stop at midday so you don't get your cute little nose burned."

Gussie giggled. She bet the man had met his match in her youngest sister, and he didn't even know it.

Rafe felt high color filling his cheeks. "It don't take a genius to know your kind, or yours either." He turned toward Gussie, his jaw set in pure, unadulterated anger. His eyes narrowed into slits, dark brows knit together above them.

"This is my fight with you." Willow jerked his arm and spun him back around to scowl up into his brown eyes. "Don't be evading the issue. You want a list of my credentials, cowboy? Well, here they are." She jerked off her gloves and held her hands out, callused palms up. "I worked in a bank for a month and then it took me almost that long to make the journey here so they're not as good a testimony as they were before that. I can build a fence all day and then go home and split a rick of wood before I cook supper and do the washing. I can build a fire in the middle of a field with nothing but cow chips for fuel and make a supper that would make your old mouth water. I can put on a calico dress and dance until the fiddler can't hold up his arms to play another tune after I spent a day working and branding cattle. My cute little nose has been sunburned in the summer when Aunt Harriet and I made hay. It's near froze off when I fed cattle in two feet of snow in the winter. So don't you judge me, Mr. Whatever-to-devil your name is. I don't care if you have angel wings under that shirt or devil's horns sprouting out your head. And yes, I can drive a team of oxen from here to California. I'm also a durned good blacksmith and a passable veterinarian for the animals."

"You got anything else to say to us?" Gypsy asked, her light eyes sparkling in amusement. "Or would you like to hear my credentials? Or how about Velvet's or the rest of them? I think we can hold our own."

"So what do you say?" Garnet grinned at Hank. She wondered if her little sister, Willow, could play the piano, too. Blast it all, that was one fine speech she'd put upon the cowboy. Garnet had seen his kind in the saloon lots of times. Swaggering in as if just being a man gave him the right to walk all over women. Well, by golly, she didn't want to go to California and get married but she'd walk the whole distance and sing a happy song while she did it to keep Mr. Whatever-the-angel his name was from winning this argument.

Willow dropped her callused hands and stared at Hank, who shook his head as if the motion would nullify the whole issue.

"What do you think?" he finally asked Rafe.

"I think you're crazier than a outhouse rat if you take these five on. We got our quota plus two. That's enough," Rafe said, talking to Hank and not backing down one blink from the staring match he was engaged in with the she-cat Jake had spawned the last time he took a wife.

"And what happens if we get there with ninety-nine or ninety-six? Someone gave good money and don't have a wife. Girls here say that if we get there with any more than a hundred, they'll step back and let the rest have the husbands first. They're just going to be our insurance. You really can drive a team, Miss Willow?" Hank asked.

"I could take this train to California by myself if I had

to," she said, still not blinking. Those were the brownest eyes she'd ever seen, and there was sorrow hidden down in the depths of them. Lots of it. More than she'd known in her lifetime. She wondered what had hardened him against women in general, and blonds in particular. She'd had her fair share of troubles, too, and she sure wasn't ready to trust a man, not after Pete Hanson's dirty trick, but she wasn't standing there telling Rafe Pierce that he wasn't any smarter than a box of rocks.

"Snippy little thing, ain't you," Hank laughed.

"Just statin' facts, Mr. Gibson; just statin' facts. Aunt Harriet said if women folks were ever going to be treated as equals to men, they had to learn to be equals. She taught me to work hard and think for myself. I'm not a simpering bag of bones and blond hair," she stated flatly.

Rafe looked over at Hank. Surely he wasn't entertaining notions of really letting these brassy women go with them. The only one who looked like she might be wife material was the one they called Velvet.

"There's one spare wagon," Hank said. "You'll have to narrow your belongings down to what will fit in one small trunk each. The rest of the wagon will be filled with supplies. Flour, a little sugar, coffee. Those things that will have to last for the five of you from here to Hollenberg Stage Station where we'll restock. You'll be responsible for driving your wagon all day, cooking your own meals, and taking care of yourselves. It's not an easy thing you're asking. And when you get to California, if there's still a hundred women, you'll have gone the whole way with no prospects of a husband or means to get back to Missouri."

"I'll take the first day of driving," Velvet said quietly. "We can each take turns."

"You can drive a team?" Gypsy asked incredulously.

"I can." Velvet nodded. "Can you?"

"Yes, I can," Gypsy said.

"Well, I can drive a buggy with a horse, but I can't drive a team," Garnet said.

"There," Rafe snorted. "Not all of them are men in dresses."

"Don't you get sassy, cowboy." Willow turned on him again, bristling up for another round. "We'll manage our wagon and our team. You just do your job and stay out of our way."

"You ain't going yet. I want a word with Hank in private," Rafe said.

"Reckon that's all right," Hank nodded. "Ladies, you wait out in the hallway. I'll think this over for ten minutes and give you my answer then."

Six chairs were lined up against the wall outside the door. Evidently, when Hank first started signing women on, there had been a waiting line. Garnet sat down, drew a fan from her reticule, and slowly moved the air around her face. What in the name of all that was sane had she just done? She wasn't about to go on this hare-brained trip with four sisters she'd only just met this morning. She wasn't cut out to be a wife or a mother. Heaven help the man who thought he could tame her enough to make either of her. But it had been so easy to stand up for Willow in there. It must be right that blood was thicker than water.

Gypsy eased her tiny frame into the chair beside Garnet. That was more fun than she'd had in months. That stupid cowboy thinking he could just come in and declare they couldn't go. Well, little sister Willow had put him in his place in a hurry. Who'd have ever thought she'd been raised up to do all those things? With that mop of blond curls and that beautiful pale skin, Gypsy had figured her for a fragile pansy.

Velvet sat down with a thud. She was medium everything. Not one beautiful thing about her, unlike her four newly found sisters. Willow was so lovely, it just plumb took a person's breath away. Gussie was tall and had thick tawny hair; Gypsy just needed a colorful scarf and she could really live up to her name, and Garnet, with her red hair and aqua eyes, was a vision. Velvet remembered the picture of a naked lady she had seen one time in the saloon when she and her little friend had peeked in the swinging doors on a dare from the town boys. Velvet had never forgotten the picture or the whipping she got later from her grandfather when he found out what she'd done. Looking back, she figured if Garnet was strip-stark naked she'd look just like that picture.

Willow's heart was racing. She hadn't had a good argument like that in months. Not since before Aunt Harriet died. Aunt Nellie and Uncle Herman were refined and never raised their voices. Why, they wouldn't holler and have a rousting good argument if it meant they had to stand before a firing squad for their lackluster lives. Willow wanted to kick the door open and march right back in there for round two. Maybe she'd win for sure and the cowboy wouldn't go on the trip with them.

In a few minutes the door flew open and Rafe Pierce stormed out. His brown eyes were drawn down in anger and his mouth was set in a firm line of pure disgust as he stopped in front of Willow. "Don't be thinkin' you've won, Willow Dulan. In a week you'll be begging to go back east. I don't believe a word of that speech in there. Not one word of it. No woman can do what you claim. So that makes you a liar."

Willow was on her feet—so close to his face she could feel the heat from his anger. "Don't you call me a liar, you sorry skunk. You don't know jack squat about me."

"I know women and there ain't a one of you worth shootin'," he said.

"Well, I know men and you're all worth shootin'. That's about all you're good for, so darlin' just load me a pistol and I'll make sure you get what you are worth," she smarted right back at him.

"You're going to regret this day. All five of you," Rafe said. "If you have a lick of common sense you'll go in there and tell Hank you changed your mind. Jake Dulan was a friend of mine. He used to tell me what worthless wives he had, and you are all your mothers' daughters, except for those eyes. All of you have his eyes. But they won't take you far when it comes to walking ten miles a day. And when you get to the end of the journey, what kind of wives will you make?"

"Well, thank goodness you won't be among the hundred men waiting for us. If you were I'd sure enough back down from this trip," Willow said.

"I think you've judged us enough," Gussie said, joining Willow and crowding Rafe backwards a step.

"Just stating facts, ma'am," he said, turning and stomping loudly down the hall to another room. He slammed the door shut with such force that it rattled the pictures on the walls.

"Guess that little altercation means we have been accepted." Velvet smiled, her face beaming with a rare beauty.

"I think it does. But that man better stay out of my sight the whole trip," Willow said.

Chapter Three

Stars twinkled in the dark sky like tiny diamonds scattered across a field of black velvet. Willow watched one fall from the heavens in a streak of glory and wondered about the miners waiting for their new brides at the end of the trip. Would a hundred women still be alive—or would she have to stand up beside one of those men and promise to love him until death? She shuddered at that thought. She had no intention of ever marrying, not after that fiasco in Mercersburg.

She readjusted her pillow and looked around her at the campfires, glowing all the way back to St. Joseph. People waited impatiently for their turn to cross the river. Tomorrow, Hank's last four wagons would go across and catch up to the others. Rafe Pierce, who'd drawn the job of bringing up the rear, had stayed behind to ride with them. If there was a God up there among all those stars he sure had a ferocious sense of humor. Of all the men who'd be working alongside Hank, Rafe would be the one to draw the short straw to ride at the tail end of the train.

To make matters worse, as luck would have it, their wagon was the last one in the line. Hank had explained his reasons at the meeting they'd had night before last. "The first women to sign on will be the first ones in the line.

Seems only right and fitting that way. Five women to the wagon. Might be a little cramped if the weather gets bad but other than that, everyone will sleep outside anyway. Starting tonight. We'll gather up by the river. Tomorrow we start across. Don't know if we'll all make it or not, but if we don't, Rafe Pierce, here, will stay behind and bring those that don't get across on the next mornin'. We'll go slow and you'll catch up by nightfall."

His words echoed in Willow's mind as she wondered what in the devil she was doing lying out in the open with nineteen other women waiting to cross the Missouri River the next morning. What she should be doing was gathering her calico skirt around her and lighting a shuck back into St. Joseph. She could find some kind of work. Like Velvet said that first day, she could always work as a maid in the hotel. Or, if the local blacksmith wasn't real prejudiced against women, she could get a job there. It was hot, sweaty work, but at least there wouldn't be a man demanding his rights as a husband at the end of the day.

Willow shut her eyes, willing herself to go to sleep. It didn't work so she squeezed them tighter. She wouldn't think about the end of the journey. She'd only think about the trip itself and getting to know her four sisters. As different as wildflowers in a field they all were, and yet there was something similar among them, too. Willow couldn't put her finger on it, not in a lifetime. However, it bound them together into a formidable Dulan force.

Her breath caught in the middle of her chest when she felt the presence of someone—or something—too close to her. Willow wrapped her fingers around the pistol under the covers beside her right leg, easing her trigger finger into place. It might just be a possum staring at her with its beady little eyes, but Willow knew better than to take chances. It might be a two-legged skunk trying to rob them of what meager belongings they'd put in the wagon to haul all the way to California.

* * *

She was a pretty little thing lying there on the hard ground; she reminded Rafe of another woman. But that was a lifetime ago, even if it did seem like only yesterday at times. More than five years had built a hard layer of scar tissue around his heart. He felt sure that no one could melt the icicles from the pits of his soul. Most especially a spitfire, high-tempered blond-haired woman. A slow grin tickled the corners of his mouth as he thought about the argument they'd had. He hadn't allowed himself that much emotion in so long he'd forgotten the last time. Could it have really been five years ago?

A big black spider made its way slowly from the grass to the edge of Willow's pallet. A notion flitted through Rafe's mind to see how long it would take before the spider crawled across her bedroll, and used those blond tresses as a bridge to her face. He'd be willing to lay odds it wouldn't be more than a few seconds before she was howling loud enough to wake up the rest of the women. It might be worth it to see her humbled a bit. Wasn't a woman alive who wasn't deathly afraid of spiders. At least that's what Katy had told him.

The spider inched along cautiously. No, he couldn't make the other women lose a night's sleep because one stupid blond got bit by a spider. He reached down to brush it off the pallet and step on it with the toe of his boot. Suddenly, he found himself looking into the barrel end of a pistol. Willow's eyes were wide open, staring at him with such icy anger that it chilled him in spite of the warm night air.

"What do you think you're doing, cowboy?" she asked without a single quiver in her voice.

"Killing a spider before it bites you and we have to listen to you moan and groan for days," Rafe said. "Put that gun away."

"I don't believe you," Willow said levelly, with no intentions of putting her gun down. She did ease the itching trigger finger back a fraction of an inch, though.

"There it is," Rafe said, shifting his eyes toward the spider that was about to crawl across her lap.

"You just stand up real slow and back up six feet," Willow said. "And don't get any funny notions either, cowboy, or I'll put a hole through your sorry heart so fast you won't even have time to make peace with your Maker before you're staring Him in the eyeballs."

Rafe set his mouth in a firm line and did what she said. Mercy, but she was a piece of work. He pitied the man who had to marry her at the end of the line. The poor fool might as well take that gun and blow his brains all over California because he was in for a life of pure misery.

When Rafe was a safe distance away, Willow glanced down at the spider. The huge black hairy thing was as big as an elephant and one bullet wouldn't come close to killing it, she was sure. It took every bit of willpower she had not to jump up, scream herself hoarse, and do a war dance around the campsite until someone killed the monster. But that's what Rafe Pierce wanted her to do, so he could laugh at her. No, this was test number one and she'd pass it or she'd never hear the end of it.

She hated spiders. No, she detested spiders. Aunt Harriet had made her kill her own spiders from the time she was five years old. But she'd never gotten over the rush of fear that filled her breast every time she saw one.

Willow laid her gun to the side and picked up the light sheet that had covered her body, wrapping the spider up in the middle of it. There was no way she was going to squash something that big and then have its remains in a dark blob on top of her all night long. When she had the monster wrapped securely in the sheet she stood up, took it to the campfire, and shook the sheet over the top. The spider didn't even sizzle when it hit the hot coals. It just shriveled up and disintegrated. "I'd think you should be getting some sleep, too, cowboy. We might be women but we can sure enough take care of ourselves. We don't need you to keep big mean spiders away from us."

Rafe just stared in amazement as she picked up her gun and lay back down on the pallet. "I can see that," he said. "Good night, Willow Dulan. Just because you killed a spider doesn't mean I've changed my mind about you."

"Honey, it'd take a lot more than you saving me from a spider to make me change my mind about you," she said. "You're still just an egotistical man. Good night, Rafe Pierce."

Stay out of my life, Rafe Pierce, she thought as she tucked her gun under the covers with a hand shaking almost as bad as her heart and soul.

Chapter Four

"What hat was that little incident with Rafe Pierce last night?" Gypsy asked the next morning over breakfast. "I thought for a minute I was dreaming, then when I opened my eyes you were squared off with him. Lord, girl, where'd that gun come from so fast?"

"I keep it handy. Never know what will happen." Willow dished up scrambled eggs topped with crumbled bacon and cheese. "Better eat them slow. Won't be no more until we get to some Indian mission up the trail and maybe not until we get to the Hollenberg Station. Might even be the last we see until we get to California, since we're the last wagon. All the others will get to every stop before we do. All we'll see is the leftovers."

Velvet sighed. "And I do like eggs for breakfast. What do you figure we'll be having?"

"Pancakes with no butter and homemade sugar syrup," Willow said.

"Sounds all right by me. I'm not much for breakfast," Garnet said. "I usually sleep until noon after playing the piano all night."

"You do what?" Willow asked.

"Play the piano," Garnet said. "Tell you what. We got us a little while before those two ferries come back for us.

They got to take the first two wagons and then us so we'll visit a spell. We've talked about this trip and we've talked some about Jake Dulan but none of us have said much about why we were so eager to come to St. Joseph. I'll go first while we wait. My mother was the one who died from a rattlesnake bite. I was raised by my grandmother. I'm twenty-two years old and I've been on my own for six years. Started out working for an aunt in her dress shop then figured out I had a hand for the piano. Been playing the last four years in a two-bit hotel lobby. To be honest, it was The Silver Spur in Little Rock. Some folks might call it a hotel. There's rooms upstairs and I had one that belonged to me. But no men visited me in that room—I just want you to know that. But I did play a mean piano for a lot of whiskey-drinking men until the wee hours of the morning. That's why I didn't get out of bed until noon most days. Guess that will all change now, though, won't it? Here we sit, eating the last of the eggs we're going to see for months and months, and the sun is just barely rising. For three days past eternity we'll be getting up before the sun and then when we get to California, I'm sure our wonderful husbands ain't going to let us lay up in bed until noon every day." Garnet smoothed the front of her calico dress. It had a dark blue background with little red flowers with yellow centers. By the time they reached California it would no doubt be faded. The flowers would be a sick pink and the threadbare fabric would be the color of a summer sky. Willow eyed her older sister. She was truly the most beautiful redhead Willow had ever seen. No freckles and translucent skin that would befit any Southern belle. Her voice was soft and yet there was a no-nonsense quality when she told them no men ever visited her room.

"Well, my mother was the preacher's daughter," Velvet said. "When she died, I went to live with my grandparents. I'm twenty-one years old and I came here from South Carolina. A few months ago my grandfather decided I was getting long in the tooth and needed a husband. He made arrangements with a widowed deacon to come calling on me. The man is twenty years older than I am and has a daughter just a couple of years younger. I finally got up the nerve to tell Grandfather I wasn't going to marry the man the same day the summons came from Jake. Grandfather said I'd stay in South Carolina and marry him or I'd just as well go on to find Jake because I wouldn't be welcome in his house. So I guess I'm with Garnet. I didn't leave anything behind to go back to. I don't know why in the world I'm going on this train. I just hope when we reach the end of the journey there's enough women so that I don't have to marry someone I don't even know." She smiled.

It was the smile, Willow decided. Until her sister Velvet smiled she was just an ordinary, plain looking woman. Medium height, medium brown hair, the crystal clear aqua-blue eyes that they all had. But nothing spectacular until a smile lit up her face like a fireworks display.

"Well, you will." Rafe stepped out from behind the wagon where he'd been listening to the sisters. Their calm acceptance of each other intrigued him. He'd have sworn there would be fireworks among them after he had read the letter from their father.

"I told you we can take care of ourselves," Willow bowed up to him. "What are you doing eavesdropping on a private conversation, anyway?"

"I came to tell you to get things ready. We'll be loading your wagon in thirty minutes. The first two got across faster than we expected. They're putting the next to the last one on the ferry now and you'll go next. Get this all cleaned up and ready, or I'll be most happy to leave you behind, ladies." He tipped his hat and moved out into the semi-darkness.

"If I didn't know better, I'd think he's got his eye on you, Willow," Gypsy whispered with a giggle.

"Probably just to make sure she doesn't shoot him in the back," Gussie laughed deeply from the bottom of her chest.

"Willow ain't got time for no two-bit wagon runner like him."

"Amen." Willow nodded, picking up the skillet and scrubbing it out with a bit of salt. In less than five minutes, all five of them had their bedrolls tucked into the wagon and were waiting for Rafe to come back.

"I'll go next," Gussie said. "I'm the oldest of the bunch of us. My given name's Augusta but I've always gone by Gussie. My grandparents kept me a while, I suppose. I wouldn't remember that far back. I was shoved from pillar to lamp post all of my growing up years. A few months with this cousin. A few with that aunt. A little while with a great aunt. When I turned sixteen, I struck out on my own. Tried being a maid for some rich folks, but decided what I really wanted to do was dance. I've been doing just that for the past five years. Dancing in a saloon. I had a room upstairs. Like Garnet said, it was my room and I got paid good enough I didn't have to entertain menfolks up there after hours. I reckon I can get a job about anywhere there's a saloon. I'm good at what I do and I brought my costumes with me. Tell the truth, I don't care if I end up married or not. If I don't I'll just find me a dance hall with a stage. If I do, well, I've always had a hankering for a bunch of kids that I can love like I wasn't."

Imagining Gussie in a short dancing dress wasn't difficult for Willow to do, but it was evident that Velvet was aghast at such an idea. Willow sucked in a lungful of air to tell her story but Gypsy beat her to it.

"I'm Gypsy Rose from south Texas. Momma was a Mexican lady and my Grandpapa about had a fit when she married Jake Dulan. At least that's what my Aunt Rosa says. I'm twenty years old. Practically an old maid and all I've ever done is work on a ranch. My Aunt Rosa and Uncle Jose have a horse ranch and I've lived with them since I was five years old. Uncle Jose has paraded the men in front of me for years, but none of them suit me. I don't know why. They just don't. Aunt Rosa and Uncle Jose weren't happy about me coming to see Jake. They thought he was a good-for-nothing gold digger when he married my mother. I don't know if I'd go back or not," she said with a shrug of her shoulders.

Willow prepared again to relate her own story.

"Well, I'm Willow and I'm the biggest disappointment he had because I was just another girl and he didn't even like my mother when it was all said and done," she said. "But I'll be hanged from the nearest oak tree with a worn-out rope if I set foot on a stagecoach back to Pennsylvania. I'll dance with Gussie first. I was raised since I was five by my Great-Aunt Harriet. She was a no-nonsense woman full of spit and vinegar. Never did marry and didn't have any intentions of a man telling her how to run her ranch. She died last year. Farm was tied up in some kind of legal thing that said Aunt Harriet could live there her whole life if she didn't marry but at her death it went back to her brother, Uncle Herman. Anyway, Uncle Herman and Aunt Nellie decided to sell the farm, but they offered me a place with them until I could find a husband. Uncle Herman is the town banker and neither he nor Aunt Nellie liked me very much. But what can I say—the feeling was certainly mutual. I worked at the bank some, but it sure wasn't what I'd want to do the rest of my life. When the summons came from Jake, Aunt Nellie and her husband gave me an ultimatum: *Leave if you want to but if you do don't never come back.* I just can't believe Jake didn't at least tell us about each other."

"I guess I wouldn't mind a husband and kids." Velvet nodded seriously. "I really do want a good husband to love me and take care of me. I just don't want him to be shoved at me and I sure don't want him to have kids as old as me."

"In five years I'll be past my prime dancing years. Drinking men don't want to see an old woman up on the stage dancing. They want something young and fresh," Gussie said. "So I suppose I'd be willing to settle down with a husband sometime or another if there ain't enough women when we get there. If there is, then I'll just dance out my five years and find someone then. And we'll have the fun of the journey and getting to know each other."

"I want a tall blond god." Gypsy laughed. "Who fills out the backside of his jeans well and has muscles that bulge his shirt sleeves. You find me that man and I'll do the rest."

"I don't want to even think about a husband." Garret shook her head. "All men are the same. Didn't Jake prove that to us? I'll just play my piano until I'm too old and think about the rest of it then. So you all better sure enough hope there's a hundred women when we get there. I'm just along for the journey and to get to know the bunch of you."

"You're crazy." Gussie giggled. "Rafe would tell Hank in a split second to put you off the train if he heard that."

"Heard what?" Rafe asked. "What is it that I'm not supposed to hear?"

"Not one thing, cowboy. You always sneakin' around listenin' to our conversations? You might ought to be careful. You could hear something that'll burn your sweet little ears," Gypsy said sweetly.

"You ready?" Rafe asked gruffly.

"Honey, you just tell Willow what to do. She's driving today. And then get out of our way," Gypsy said, her blue eyes twinkling.

"You better stay out of my way. I'd still like to leave you at any wayside station between here and Ash Hollow," he said.

"Why Ash Hollow? Why not all the way to California?" Gussie asked.

Willow climbed up in the wagon seat and flicked the reins over the backs of four big, healthy oxen. She strained her ear to hear his answer, though, and then got furious at herself for even caring what Rafe Pierce had to say.

"Because that's where I leave you ladies to yourselves. Tavish O'Leary takes my spot then. I'll be more than ready to give the job to him. If I'd known Hank would sign on you five I'd never have agreed to come along—even for the first leg," he said curtly as he mounted his horse and nodded to Willow to follow him.

"I like it." Gypsy laughed. "I love it. We only have to put up with the sourpuss for a month. Then we go to California to look at the rich men. If we don't like them when we get there ain't nobody big enough to hogtie us and make us marry them. Besides, there might be a big old Swede there. One that at least looks like a blond god."

"I don't know," Velvet said. "It still scares me, some. To go all that way and marry men we've never even met. How could you live with a man you don't even know?"

"Never know the sorry rascals until you live with them," Garnet said. "That's why I don't never intend to marry or live with one. It's against the law to shoot 'em." Garnet grinned, showing off beautiful even white teeth and dimples in both cheeks.

"Okay, sisters, it's time to drive this thing onto the ferry. I haven't ever done that so you'd better say a prayer back there," Willow said. "We got to work hard to prove that sorry rascal wrong."

"A bossy thing, ain't you? Bet you got that from Jake Dulan," Gussie said.

"Probably. Bet you got your determination from him, too," Willow said.

"Yes, I'm sure we all did," Gypsy chimed in. "Isn't this exciting?"

"Tell me that in three months, when we've walked the soles off two pairs of boots and we're brown as Indians." Gussie groaned at the idea.

"I'm already that brown," Gypsy said. "How much money do you have left? I have enough to buy three extra pairs of walking boots at the stations if there's any left when we get to them."

Willow shook her head and guided the oxen onto the ferry with enough finesse that Rafe grunted his disappointment. He would have liked to see her tumble the wagon and all its contents into the river. Then he could take the other fifteen women and their three wagons on to Hank and tell him fate had declared after all that the Dulan women weren't supposed to be on this train.

The river water looked cold but there wasn't room on the ferry for Rafe and his horse, so he'd just show Willow Dulan now tough he was. He whispered into his horse's ear, promising him a big portion of oats along with a whole handful of sugar lumps if he'd just swim across the river . . . very fast! Rafe bit the inside of his full mouth when the cold water rushed through the legs of his jeans and chilled him to the bone. *Cold* didn't come close to describing this river on the last day of April. *Icy* barely got the idea across.

He kept his distance a few feet behind the ferry, keeping his eyes on the far shore, hoping he hadn't completely frozen the lower half of his legs plumb off by the time old Buster climbed up out of the water. He saw a log floating toward them but paid no attention to it. A fallen tree, probably struck by lightning last month when the spring storms swept over the plains. He didn't see the water moccasin lazing on the top side of the log, not until it raised its ugly head, shot its forked tongue in and out like a kid licking a lollipop, and looked old Buster right in the eye.

No amount of sweet talking could keep the horse from pitching around in the water like a fish that'd been flipped onto dry land. After he saw the snake, Buster reared up on his hind feet, pawing at the air. The log floated on past, taking the snake with it, but Rafe was tossed off the back of the horse into the shallow water.

The girls, all but Willow, witnessed the whole show from the ferry, and giggled when Rafe went off the horse's back. That would show the uppity, know-it-all cowboy that he wasn't really an angel sent from Heaven to pronounce judgment on the five of them.

"What's so funny?" Willow asked as the ferryman

brought them to the wharf. She flicked the reins, clucked her tongue, and steered the oxen onto the shore.

"Oh, that Rafe," Gypsy said. "His horse just flipped him out into the water. He thinks he's so big and important."

"He's not coming up," Velvet said nervously.

"Oh, it's shallow there." Garnet wiped at her eyes.

"He should be up by now." Velvet wrung her hands.

"Yep, he should," Gussie agreed.

Willow snorted as she rapidly tore off her skirt and shirt-waist and tossed them in the back of the wagon. She should let Rafe drown after the attitude he'd given her, but she wasn't sure she could ever expect to get into Heaven if she allowed a man with an angel's name to die in the water. Funny, wasn't he the one who was supposed to be stirring up the water and healing folks?

"What are you doing?" Garnet asked.

"Saving his sorry hide. Where'd he go under?" Willow said, drawing in a lungful of air and getting ready to jump into the cold water.

"Right there. A few feet from that log. Oh, look at that snake!" Velvet said tremulously.

"Snake!" Willow didn't look. The only thing in the world worse than a spider was a rotten snake. They were all poisonous. She didn't care what Aunt Harriet said about some of them being good snakes. Willow's opinion was that the only good snake was a dead one. Dead and buried at that. Even dead ones with their head severed from their old wiggly bodies were evil. She plunged into the icy water, pushing the snake from her mind.

The water was so murky she couldn't see anything but she stayed under, groping for anything, until she thought her lungs would explode. Mercy, as big as that cowboy stood and as tall as he sat in the saddle, you'd think she could grab hold of some part of his body. Finally she had to surface to refill her lungs, and on the way up something brushed the inside of her arm. Willow grabbed for it and brought it to the top with her. It felt like a man's arm, but if it was just a raft for another snake, she might be joining Rafe Pierce at the pearly gates before the morning was finished.

She came up out of the water in a rush, gasping for air and bringing Rafe with her. Blood streamed down his wet face and he was as still as death. The other four girls, along with the ferryman, helped bring him to shore, where Willow flipped him over on his stomach and commenced to pumping river water from his lungs. She counted, "One, two three," and then with all the force she could muster bore down on his back, right under his shoulder blades. After four times he began to empty his lungs. Willow didn't let up, but kept on until he moaned and gasped, trying to find the oxygen he'd lost.

"Looks like he's going to live if he don't bleed to death," the ferryman said. "You girls got things under control now? I got a whole day's work bringing the wagons across so I'll leave you to it."

"Just like a man," Garnet said when he'd walked away. "Ain't that just dandy. We got a bleeding man who's hardly conscious and four wagons to get to the others by dark. Let's hope they cut a wide swath through the grass that we can follow."

"Willow said she could take this train to California by herself," Gussie said.

"Help me get Rafe to the wagon so I can sew his head up." Willow sighed. "And I expect that if Velvet will drive a spell today, I can ride that horse over there and take us right to Hank."

"You can sew that up?" Garnet shuddered.

"Can't be much different than sewing up a horse. At least he's still out and won't be kicking around, carrying on. You get his legs and me and Gussie will haul his shoulders." She motioned for Gypsy and Garnet to grab hold of Rafe's soaking jeans.

Willow searched around in her trunk until she found her medicine bag. She took out a curved needle, ran it through the flame from a candle to sterilize it, and carefully threaded it. She cleaned the wound as best she could, then poured a healthy amount of whiskey into it before she started stitching it together. The good-looking Rafe Pierce would now have a nice, two-inch scar right in the middle of his forehead. Not that it would make a penny's worth of difference to any woman past thirteen. He'd still be rakishly handsome.

"Yuk." Garnet scrunched up her nose.

"Oh, not so bad," Velvet said. "I'm just glad Willow can do it, though. I could if I had to, but it always makes me a bit squeamish to actually stick the needle in someone's skin. I can help by holding the person's hand but sewing up skin isn't so easy." She guided the wagon to where the other three waited already in a line.

"We've had an accident," Gussie told the waiting women. "Rafe Pierce fell off his horse and was knocked out in the water. Looks like he hit his head on a rock. Willow saved him and is sewing him up. So if you ladies will follow me, I guess we'll go it on our own today. We should catch up with the train by nightfall."

"No," one woman said flatly. "I'm Constance, and I say we wait for Mr. Pierce to guide us, just like we were told."

"And I say," Willow poked her head out the back of the wagon, "that Rafe Pierce ain't going to be able to do a blessed thing for a while. If he can sit a horse in a week, we'll be lucky. So, you going to sit here and moan, Miss Constance, or you going to follow this wagon? Because we're going on, with or without you all."

"We're going," another woman nodded. "How hard can it be, anyway?"

"I don't like it," Constance declared.

"Nobody said you got to like it," the other woman said. "All you got to do is follow that wagon just like the girl said." She walked back to the wagon, drew back the sheeting, and peeked inside. "When you get that job done, Missy, you put some clothes on. Don't need no talk going around that you spent the day in the wagon with a man in your unmentionables. Won't be no husband waiting on you if that gets out. Rest of you will keep your mouth shut and we'll do just what this lady said." She motioned toward Gussie.

"Thank you. Velvet, drive 'em up front and follow the grass trail best you can until Willow can get on that horse and scout for us. My name is Gussie Dulan. These are my four sisters. Willow, in there sewing up our guide. Garnet and Gypsy right here. And Velvet driving."

"I'm Annie," the woman said. "Annie Wilson. We might be women but we ain't stupid, in spite of what most men-folks think."

"I like you, Annie." Gussie smiled. "Now let's go. We've wasted half an hour or more saving Willow's angel."

"I heard that!" Willow shouted from inside the wagon.

Chapter Five

The slow burn in Rafe's chest and the ache in his head jerked him out of unconsciousness. When he opened his eyes, he couldn't believe the sight. There stood Rachel in nothing but her dripping wet underwear, which was sticking to her like a second skin. Her long blond hair hung down her back in limp curls. He took stock of his surroundings: several trunks lined up over there where Rachel was putting something away, a makeshift bedroll on the floor where he lay, boxes of supplies. Good grief, where was the girl taking him and why did she hit him over the head to get him here? Unless he was stark raving mad, this was a covered wagon. Rachel wouldn't be traveling in such a style and besides, where did all those curls come from? Rachel's hair was long, straight, and was like pure silk when he twined his fingers in it. He didn't want to be in a wagon with Rachel. Not now. Not five years after she'd played him for the biggest fool in all of Nebraska. Where was Katy? She'd take care of it.

"Katy," he coughed, then moaned in pain.

"Who?" Willow turned quickly to see if he was coming back to life or joining up with the real angels in Heaven.

"Katy, please," Rafe mumbled just as his eyes fluttered and shut again.

Willow wanted nothing more than to grab him, shake him back into the real world, put him on that big black beast of a horse, and make him do his job. But it didn't look like things were going to be that simple. Well, one thing for durned sure, she wasn't about to lead her four wagons through the deep spring grass riding astride his horse in a dress. No, siree, and if one of those other women, including her four sisters, had a problem with the way she intended to dress, they could just swallow their feminine pride and shut their prissy mouths. She pulled a pair of well-worn overalls and a flannel shirt from her trunk, glanced over her shoulder to make sure Rafe's eyes really were closed, and peeled off her wet underthings, dropping them on the floor of the wagon. The soft flannel shirt felt better than anything she'd had on in months and the overalls, though a bit looser than the last time she'd worn them, felt like faithful old friends. She dug to the bottom of the trunk and found a pair of leather boots Aunt Harriet had commissioned the boot maker to produce especially for her small feet. She pulled on a pair of socks and then jammed her feet down into the brown leather boots.

"Well, Rafe Pierce, you just lay right there and sleep, darlin'. Have sweet dreams about your Katy, who-ever-the devil she is, and I'll do your job for you," she said sassily as she hung her wet things over the five trunks to dry.

"Oh, my," Constance sputtered when Willow threw back the wagon sheet and stepped outside. "That's not at all proper. What would the future husbands think if they saw you like that?"

"Honey, we're already behind since we had to stop and pump river water out of our scout's lungs and sew up his head. The future husbands are at least six months down the road, maybe longer. I don't imagine their eyesight can reach all this far," Willow said. "Now I'm going to ride that horse out in front of these four wagons. Until we join up with Hank our wagon is going to be right behind me. I don't give a royal rat's hind end how the rest of you line it up, but I want Rafe close enough so that if I'm needed to take care of him I can hear Velvet whistle."

"Yes, ma'am." Annie stepped up. "My wagon will bring up the rear until we join up with the others. And Miss Willow, I think you are a brave woman. I'm glad you were here to help us. Now let's get these wagons rolling, ladies. We're wasting good light. You think we'll catch up to them by nightfall?"

"I hope so," Willow hefted herself up onto Rafe's horse and settled into the saddle. By nightfall, she'd be walking bowlegged and feel like she had a barrel permanently between her knees, but by golly, they'd be closer to catching up with the other wagons than if they'd sat beside the river and wrung their hands all day.

Rafe drifted in and out of semi-consciousness all morning and up into the afternoon. He would almost conquer the dense gray fog surrounding him, then just as his eyes fluttered, he'd sink back into a world where he couldn't get his thoughts in line. First there was the rocking motion of a coach or a wagon; then there was Rachel, but where was Katy? She promised she'd never let the woman back on his ranch. Why had Rachel kidnapped him? She didn't want him five years ago, so why'd she want him now? Was he alive or had he died and neither destiny wanted him for all eternity? Each question had an answer somewhere, but they were hiding in the thick fog just outside his reach.

Tall green grass grew in the ruts the wagon wheels had made but it was crushed so well that Willow didn't have a problem leading the four wagons. The horse wasn't nearly as frisky or mean as old Lucifer had been. Lord, now, there was a horse that could make her break out in hives at the thought of riding him. Only Aunt Harriet could tame that beast, and she did it, to the chagrin of half the men in Mercersberg, Pennsylvania. She smiled, remembering Aunt Harriet: ninety percent bluff, ten percent mean. No one in Mercersberg ever wanted to be on the other side of the fight if she wasn't bluffing. Willow wondered if she was just like Aunt Harriet. Only ten percent mean?

"Not on your life," she said to herself. "I've got more than that. After all, I'm the last begotten daughter of Jake Dulan. That ups my percentage by at least ten more points."

"Were you talking to me?" Velvet asked from the wagon seat.

"No, just mumbling," Willow said.

"Looks like we might be in for a storm," Velvet said.

Willow shaded her eyes with the back of her hand. That's all she needed. A blasted spring storm. Well, they'd sure enough keep riding and walking until they had to stop and that was a fact. If there was a storm, then Hank and the rest of the train would also be stopped by it so they wouldn't get too far ahead of them.

At noon, Violet handed Willow a cold biscuit stuffed with leftover bacon from their breakfast meal. The big black clouds had obliterated the sun and a chilly breeze had picked up, sweeping across the tall grass, making it dance gracefully. Annie, Constance, and the rest of the women drew their shawls tightly around their shoulders and tied their bonnets securely around their chins. Their skirts swept from one side to the other as the fickle wind changed its mind, blowing first one way and then another.

Willow was out ahead of the four lonesome-looking little wagons making up their pitiful train when the first big drops of rain splattered across her face. She turned in the saddle to see the wagons still coming on and the women bracing themselves against the wind. If she hurried back to them they might at least get the wagons circled up before they all got wet. But then again, the rain wasn't that cold so they could keep moving and it would pass right over them. They'd be wet, but they'd dry out when the sun came back out. It was her call and Rafe would be meaner than a constipated cougar no matter what she decided. But this wasn't about Rafe Pierce. It was about twenty women who didn't have a bit of business getting soaked to the skin and catching their death of pneumonia.

"Circle 'em up, ladies," she called as she rode hell for leather back to the wagons. "We'll wait out the storm right here."

"Yes, ma'am," Annie yelled above the first serious clap of thunder. "Leave the oxen harnessed up and make a square, ladies," she said. "Hurry up now and we might make it inside before the rain hits."

"It's coming fast," Willow yelled, as she tied Rafe's horse to the back of their wagon and jumped inside with her four sisters, who were already finding places to sit.

Lightning flashed through the air in streaks, so close that Garnet swore it was trying to part her hair. Thunder grumbled and growled and the rain came down in sheets as thick as the fog Rafe slept in. Behind closed eyes he saw light somewhere beyond the fog and wanted so badly to walk toward it. He heard the rumble of someone building a house close by. The sound of the hammers hitting the boards made his head ache. Why was Rachel building a house? Where was Rachel building a house?

He heard voices, laughter . . . women's voices. More than one. The noise aggravated his headache and he retreated back into the cushion of nothingness.

"So, you think he's going to live?" Garnet nodded toward Rafe.

"I hope so," Velvet said. "There's barely room for us to sit up in here with his big old lanky body stretched out over half the floor. Can you imagine if we had to sleep in here all night? I'd almost be willing to toss his carcass out in the rain just to have room to stretch my long legs out."

Gypsy giggled. "Here we are crossing the world to find husbands and talking about throwing a perfectly good man out in the rain. Doesn't make much sense, does it?"

"Ah, we wouldn't toss out Willow's angel. We'll probably be old bears tomorrow if we have to sleep stuffed in here like sardines and living on what there is left from breakfast if we don't get to fix supper, but we wouldn't dare take the chance of bad luck by throwing a real angel out in the rain," Gussie teased, her eyes sparkling with pure mischief.

"He's not my angel. I'm not even sure he's named for an angel. I don't remember nothing about no Rafe in the Bible, and dear hearts, my Aunt Harriet sure enough was one of them Bible-toting Christian women who knew her stories," Willow said.

"Yep, he's named for one," Velvet said. "Grandpa said Rafael was the angel who troubled the waters at the healing pool. Then the next person who stepped into the troubled waters got healed."

"Looks like he sure enough troubled Willow's waters," Gussie said. "Something you needed healing from, little sister?"

"Just need healing from all worthless men," Willow snapped, and pulled the wagon sheet up a bit to check the weather. Black as midnight and here it was only the middle of the afternoon. The storm wasn't going to pass anytime soon and all that glorious rain would make the bent grass stand right up again. How on earth was she going to find the way to the rest of the train?

"I think I hear a story." Gypsy smiled. "Want to share it?"

"Nope. They're all worthless. Beginning with that skunk of a father we all share and ending right here with Mr. Rafael Pierce." Willow poked him in the leg.

At the sound of his name, Rafe bolted straight up into a sitting position, stared Willow right in the eyes without blinking, and said, "What are you doing here? And where is Katy? I want Katy and I want her right now. You have no business taking me away from the ranch, Rachel. Katy is going to shoot you right between your blue eyes."

"Well, good afternoon to you too, Rafe Pierce. And just who is Rachel and who is Katy?" Willow accentuated every word with a shake of her finger in his face.

His gorgeous mouth set in a firm line; his hands knotted into tight fists. He didn't have to explain a thing to this gaggle of women Rachel surrounded herself with, and Rachel knew dang well who Katy was. She wasn't fooling him or anyone else by her crazy talk. He started to open his mouth to give her the tongue-lashing she deserved but everything went black and he fell backwards, his head hitting a soft cloud.

"Well, what was that all about?" Garnet whispered.

"Who knows? Katy must be his wife and I'd bet Rachel is an old girlfriend," Willow said. "Maybe she looked like me. He's probably got a concussion from hitting his head on a rock. He might even have brain fever."

"Maybe he needs to trouble the water and then jump in himself," Garnet said.

"The only thing he's going to trouble is womenfolks with them good looks," Gussie declared.

"But now the angel has a scar," Gypsy said mischievously.

"Ah, when that gets well, he'll just tell the women that his halo caused that little place on his head." Willow picked up the bantering.

"And probably he'll beg her to rub it because it hurts sometimes," Garnet said.

"Yeah, right." Willow looked outside again. "And if she's wise she'll drown herself in those silly troubled waters. Or better yet, she'll drown him."

The sun set in a blazing display of oranges, pinks, and yellows, with a brilliant rainbow to dress up the scene. There they sat, four little wagons, twenty women, and one delusional man. They unhitched the oxen and staked them out to feed on the tender spring grass, Willow unsaddled Rafe's big black horse and tied him close to the Dulan wagon. She kept telling herself they'd be fine. There hadn't been an uprising of Indians in a long time, according to Hank during his little pep talk that last night. Mercy, was it only two nights ago? Seemed like a lifetime. She stood outside the hustle and bustle as the women made a communal fire in the middle of the square and brought out food to fix supper. They were laughing and getting to know each other. Gussie and Annie seemed to be the leaders in the bunch; Garnet, the funny one with her brilliant red hair and wit; Velvet, the quiet one taking care of the organization of the meal; Gypsy, everywhere at once; and that whiny Constance. *Lord,* Willow prayed silently, *don't let there be any more like her on this train. She would tax the patience of St. Peter himself with all her whining and airs.*

"Katy . . ." Rafe fretted in his sleep.

Willow slung a leg over the tailgate of the wagon and, with a little hop, she was beside him. She laid her hand gently on his forehead. No fever. Must be a concussion. Aunt Harriet said that a person suffering from a bump on the head like that could be afflicted for days, or suddenly just wake up lucid as the moment before the accident. Willow stared down at Rafe's fine form. At least his clothing had dried before the storm hit. She sure didn't look forward to undressing him and enduring the teasing of her sisters or the clucking of the rest of the women's tongues. She'd about caused a riot with her overalls and boots as it was. But, even Aunt Harriet, pious as she was, knew a woman could scarcely do a man's work tangled up in petticoats and long skirts. Until they reached the rest of the train, these women would just have to get used to her in overalls and flannel shirt. She smiled, a bit crooked, one side of her small bow-shaped mouth turning up just a fraction more than the other.

What would I find if I did undress you, Rafe Pierce? she thought, her strange aqua eyes sparkling. *Would I find wings? Or would I find a wolf in sheep's clothing? Are you a devil in disguise or a descendant of the fellow who stirred up the waters? And who in the devil is Katy?*

"So is your angel still alive?" Gussie whispered, pulling back the wagon sheet.

Willow chuckled. "If he's an angel, then he's Katy's angel. Not mine. Every time he mumbles anything it's just her name. And yes, he's still alive. No fever yet. If he makes it to morning with none, he'll probably sneak past it. Looks like he's just suffering from a big bump on the head."

"Well, come on out and visit. We're making a community stew for supper. Velvet is organizing the whole thing. Some of the girls brought out some dried beef she's boiling in a pot, along with some potatoes. After today, it sounds right fetching, I'm here to tell you," Gussie said.

Willow nodded. She'd just stepped out onto the ground and sniffed the clean, cool air when she caught a whiff of something else. Onions or garlic. One or the other, she was sure of it, and close enough that the gentle breeze brought it right to her nose. She leaned into it and sniffed again. Less than twenty yards out she found a stand of wild garlic.

"Now this will season up that pot of soup just fine." Willow gathered an armload, carrying it like firewood. "And we can dry the rest for later on." When she turned around to retrace her footsteps back to camp she saw a small clump of asparagus. She almost danced a jig right there in the middle of the plains. Then she realized the significance of what she was looking at. If Hank's wagons had come this way, they would have flattened the asparagus and the garlic. Had she brought them the wrong way? Rafe was going to have a fit seen only in the back forty of hell's acres if she'd made a grave mistake like that. She shook off the feeling of dismay. He could just have a fit. If he'd been the kind of horseman he should've been, then he wouldn't have fallen into the water. She wouldn't have had to rescue him or make good her word that she could lead this train all the way to California on her own.

"Willow." Gypsy's voice cut through the evening breeze. "Where are you?"

"Gathering garlic for the stew and asparagus for a side dish," Willow called back to her. No need to worry all these women right now. Tomorrow was soon enough to panic. But something down deep in Willow's heart didn't listen as it tightened up into a knot and ached like it did the day she found out just exactly what a skunk Pete Hanson was.

"Wow." Velvet smiled beautifully when Willow dropped the garlic on the tailgate of Annie's wagon, where they were peeling potatoes. "Are we lucky or not? This is wonderful. And asparagus, too."

"How much water have we got?" Willow asked.

"There's a big jug in each wagon. Enough for drinking and supper. Maybe a little bit for a wash basin before we go to sleep if we all share," Gussie said. "Forget a nice long bath in a tub with bubbles on the top and a big old bath sheet to wrap around your wet little body."

"You can hush." Willow giggled, easing some of the tension from her heart. "I'd give my eye teeth and one arm for a bath tonight. So don't you even talk like that."

"Would you give your angel in there?" Gussie teased.

"Honey, I'd shoot him just for the target practice. Nobody'd take a plain old man over something as wonderful as a good hot bath after a day like we've all had," Willow retorted.

"Don't sound like you're going to make a very good wife, if you ask me." Constance sniffed into the air, sticking her pert little nose so high that another downpour of rain would surely have drowned her.

Willow's eyes widened at the snippy, prissy young woman. She clasped her hands to keep from reaching out and slapping Constance's rosy little cheeks until they were blaze red. How dare she pass down judgment like that? The whole camp grew silent, waiting, watching.

"Honey, what kind of wife I make ain't one bit of your sweet little business. What is your business right now is to learn to control your mouth so it don't get you into more trouble than your scrawny hind end can get you out of. Now, you've got to live with the rest of us for a long time, since we're always going to be the last four wagons in the line, so I'd suggest you keep your hateful comments to yourself," Willow said, her eyes dancing with anger.

"You're coarse and more man than woman," Constance said. "I feel sorry for the man who gets you."

"Well, darlin', you better sharpen up your claws if you're antsing for a catfight. I don't usually engage in petty fights but honey, I don't back down from nothing. So you can either put up or shut up. I'm not living for nine months with you pecking at me like I was the littlest chickie in the pen. So it's up to you. We going to be civil or we going to pull hair and settle this right here and now? Matter of fact, after we've been in Bryte, California for six months, me and you will have a set down and discuss the finer points of being married and we'll see who does the better job."

"I ain't spoilin' for no fight with you." Constance stamped her foot and stormed off to the farthest corner of the camp. How dare that Willow Dulan talk down to her like that! A good old fist-slinging, hair-pulling fight would have been better than being laughed at. She'd show all of them. When they got to California she'd be the best wife there. She shuddered at that idea. Children . . . a man in her bed at night, Nothing could be more repulsive. By the time she was forty she'd be old, worn-out and gray-haired with nothing but kids and grandkids around her, demanding more and more of her. But there was nothing for her in St. Joseph anymore. The middle child in a family of nine girls, she'd grown tired of the poor existence of a farmer's daughter. Pretty as a picture, she'd turned down three offers of marriage. She wasn't going to scrap out a living from the earth the rest of her life. Then there was the flyer on the general store window. She could have an adventure. Go to California. Marry a gold miner. It sounded so wonderful until right at that moment.

"Hey, girl." Willow was so close behind her Constance could still smell the garlic on her skin. "We might as well get along. You know it. We'll just let bygones be bygones.

You don't know how long I've lived in these overalls and boots. And I don't know about you, but I do know you gotta be hungry, so come on over to the fire, and let's have some supper. It can get lonely on a nine-month trip without friends."

Constance sniffed. "I might not like you enough to be your friend."

"And it's a cinch, honey, that right now I don't like you any better. Life's like that. You don't have to like me, but you durn sure have to live pretty close to me for a long time." Willow smiled.

"Okay. And most folks just call me Connie," she said, sniffing the air again.

She was scared out of her mind but she'd do all right, Willow decided. She'd probably be the she-coon of the whole town of Bryte before they were all old and gray, but she'd shape up in the journey. By the time she'd spent nine months and lived through Lord only knew how many disasters along the way, a man to take care of her would begin to look almighty good.

That night Willow threw her bedroll under the wagon, her slicker on the wet ground to protect her blankets from getting wet. She stared up at the twinkling stars and hoped to goodness she hadn't led them too far off the trail, and that they hadn't been following a couple of family wagons to a homestead somewhere on the plains. Rafe slept fitfully, calling out for Katy and often cursing someone named Rachel.

What would her husband look like? She wondered. Would he be as handsome as Rafe Pierce? Or would he have a mean streak and a dishonest heart like Pete Hanson had? If he did, she vowed she'd kill him graveyard dead and spend the rest of her life in prison. Nothing was worth that kind of misery.

Chapter Six

Willow awoke to horrible screaming just outside the camp. She threw back the covers and was running in that direction before any of the other women had their eyes fully open. Barely a hundred feet away from the wagons, she could see three Indians sitting on their ponies, surrounding one of the women, who continued to scream between rib-racking sobs. The moment Willow hesitated before plowing straight ahead into the middle of the fracas was so short-lived it was noticeable only to Rafe Pierce, who was right behind her.

"What in the devil is going on?" Willow yelled from a few feet back, startling all three Indians, yet not even slowing Connie's bellowing for a half a second.

"Lady, we don't want no trouble. We been telling her that. We just rode up here and found her sleeping. Figured she belonged to that little campsite and started to wake her up when she started hollerin'," one Indian said in perfect English. "Hi, Rafe. Tell these women we aren't out to scalp them or slaughter their oxen."

Rafe Pierce hadn't taken time to see who he was running along behind. He figured from the time the screaming awoke him that one of those worthless Dulan women, probably the youngest, Willow, had encountered a spider while

54

she was out taking care of her morning constitutional. He hadn't even stopped to wonder what he was doing stretched out in a wagon or why his head throbbed. One minute he was sleeping and the next he found himself tearing out across the grass in his bare feet, following one of the other hired hands toward the frightful noise.

"Morning, Abraham Dorian." Rafe nodded toward the Indian. "You can shut up now, Willow Dulan. These are good Indians, not the kind looking to remove all that gold hair."

Connie looked up at Rafe; half a scream out in the crisp morning air, the other half still in her throat, refusing to come out. "I'm not Willow Dulan!" she said shrilly, tossing her long blond hair back defiantly.

"And what made you think she was?" Willow said, off to his right.

Rafe turned quickly to see that the skinny fellow he'd figured to be one of the hired hands wasn't a man at all. It was Willow Dulan, in overalls, a flannel shirt, no shoes, and a blond braid hanging over her shoulder. Well, she needn't think she was going to dress like that, even on a wagon train. The women would be respectable and respected right up to the last minute when Hank delivered them to Bryte, California. Rafe gritted his teeth and reached up to the ache in his head, only to find a bandage.

"Figured you'd come across another big mean spider," he said, suddenly feeling weak.

"If I had I would have burned it in the fire, or stomped it to death," she said, shooting pure daggers at him.

"What about me?" Connie whined, trying to reclaim at least some of the attention she'd had.

Willow's head snapped around to see her. "I'd say you'll have a sore throat the rest of the day, hollering like that, and that you deserve it. All that carryin' on sure wasn't necessary."

"If they'd been going to kill me at least I would have warned the rest of you they were here," Connie said shortly.

"If you'd been inside the camp where you belonged, they would have just ridden by and no one would have even seen them," Rafe told her bluntly. "Go back to your wagon and get things ready to roll. Why are we still not with Hank and the rest of the train?" He turned on Willow.

"Because you darned near drowned. Your horse tossed you in the river and after we pulled your sorry hide out, we found a nasty cut that had to be sewed up. Then you were unconscious the rest of the way. Except for the few times you sat up and whined for the women in your life." Willow put her hands on her hips and geared up for another battle with the tall, good-looking Rafe Pierce, who right now looked much more like a devil than an angel.

"You mean you women decided to move on, on your own, and not wait?" he said between gritted teeth, his upper lip setting in a snarl, nostrils flaring out.

He reminded Willow of an angry young bull. She half expected him to start pawing the ground any moment with his bare feet. If he did, then he'd better just get ready for another wound on his pretty face, because she'd learned long ago that a good solid whack across the head was the only thing a young bull understood.

Instinctively, Willow glanced around for a stick in her reach. Nothing. Unless she could wrestle one of those rifles away from the Indians. She could use the butt of it to knock some well-needed sense into his thick skull. Or she could just waste one bullet and take care of his arrogance permanently.

"Well, are you going to answer me or stand there like a bump on a log?" He raised his voice and Abraham Dorian grinned.

"You were laid up half dead and fussing about a couple of women named Rachel and Katy, Rafe Pierce. We could either sit still or I could borrow your horse and follow the trail and be closer to Hank than if we'd sat still. So that's what I did. And if you don't like it, that's your problem. We aren't helpless women. Like I said, I could take this wagon to the west coast if I had to." She was so close to his nose that if she'd leaned forward they would have been in each other's arms.

"Oh, yeah, and how do I know you haven't got the four wagons so hopelessly lost that we'll never find Hank?" He didn't take his eyes from her strange aqua-colored ones. Too bad she was such a snit and had already signed a contract to marry one of the men at the end of the line. He could sure enough learn to like looking into pretty blue eyes like those.

"They're not lost," Abraham said. "Hank and the others are on their way to the Mission. Said if we saw you on our way back to tell you he was pulling out again this morning but only planning a five-mile day. Leaving an hour late and stopping an hour early if everything went well. He said to tell you he'll meet up with you at the Mission. Storm slowed them down and he figured it had done the same for you. If you stay with it today, you'll be caught up to them by supper time, Rafe."

"Hmmph." Rafe snorted. "Well, that's good news. Now get on back to your wagon and put on some decent clothing for a woman, Willow Dulan. I'll not take you the rest of the way dressed like that. It'd be a bad example for the other women. Put on a dress and your bonnet. I'm taking over from here."

"I'll wear what I want and you'd do well to remember that, Rafe Pierce. You want me to wear a dress, then you sit on that horse of yours all day and lead the way. And let me tell you something, honey, when I put my dress on for the day, then I'm not putting on my overalls again that day. So if you get sick or if you fall off the horse from exhaustion because of that head wound, I'll leave your sorry carcass beside the trail and keep walking. I won't even stop to see if you're bleeding to death," she said.

"Whew," Abraham chuckled. "Looks like you got yourself a mean squaw."

"She's not my squaw," Rafe snapped.

"And never will be, but I am mean," Willow told Abraham. "Now, you really, really want me to put on my dress and bonnet or you want me to keep my overalls and hat on? You probably could use another day of rest with a head wound like that." She turned around to find Rafe had actually taken a step backward.

"I said to put on your dress, woman. That's what I meant. Ain't no woman ever rode my horse before and they won't again. Not as long as I can open my eyes. This train leaves in thirty minutes, so tell the other women they'd better hurry their breakfast up." Rafe's jawbones were pulsing with suppressed rage.

"Nice to meet you, Mr. Dorian." Willow smiled beautifully toward the Indian on the black pony. "So sorry Connie had such a fit and gave you a scare there. Maybe our paths will cross again someday with much better beginnings."

"Perhaps." Abraham was still smiling, his dark eyes twinkling. So his friend Rafe Pierce had finally met a woman who might be able to tame him. After that problem with the blond-haired witch a few years ago, it was good to see him with some life in his eyes again. Maybe this Willow Dulan would be good for him.

"And you better not whine one time all day," Willow said, pointing at Rafe as she walked away.

He bit his tongue, letting her have the last word, and watched her for a half a minute. How could he ever have mistaken her for a man? Even in those baggy overalls she was all female.

"Looks to me like Willow Dulan is going to make you toe the line," Abraham said softly when she was out of hearing distance.

"Willow Dulan is going to learn to toe the line before we get to Ash Hollow. I'll break that woman or die trying," Rafe said.

"Dulan? Wouldn't be kin to old Jake, would she?"

"His youngest daughter. Five of them. All different mothers." Rafe stole another glance back over his shoulder.

She'd joined the rest of a knot of women who were busy consoling Connie. She began issuing orders like an army general and the women obeyed them without a word.

"Then you better have an undertaker begin the wooden box you white men like to spend your eternity inside. Because you won't break that one, Rafe Pierce. You might make her fit to share an oxen yoke with but you won't break her to do your will," Abraham said.

"There ain't a woman alive I'd want to share a yoke with," Rafe all but growled. "And if Willow Dulan was the last woman on this whole earth, I'd want to be on one end of it and her on the other. Then I'm not so sure it would be a far enough distance to keep us from tearing it to shreds."

"I'll be riding north through Nebraska in a few months, Rafe. Some business with the government in that area. I'll stop and we'll share some tobacco and talk. We'll see then who tamed who," Abraham said.

A smile finally lit up Rafe's face. "Katy and I will barbecue a steer if you'll give us some forewarning. Just you or a bunch?"

"Oh, at least ten of us. And we'll send along a smoke signal of some kind. I'll look forward to seeing Katy and her passel of kids again." Abraham reached down to shake hands with Rafe. "Now, I expect you'd better go put your boots on if you're going to lead this little bunch on to Hank. You might catch him before supper time if you keep at it. But don't fall off the horse. That spitfire squaw would probably kick your hide out of the path and laugh while the buzzards ate your eyes out."

Rafe shivered even though he knew Abraham was joking. "I'll be careful," he said seriously.

The three braves rode off toward the east and Rafe began to walk slowly through the dew-kissed grass back to the four wagons. He could smell bacon frying already and could hear the women getting their oxen hitched back up to the wagons. So General Willow had told part of them to cook and the other part to make ready to roll. That way everyone had a hot breakfast before they began the long day. He couldn't have done it any better and it chafed him to know just how little he was needed.

Willow tossed her overalls and shirt in the corner of the wagon. When they stopped that night, if there was water nearby, she'd wash them before storing them back in her trunk. Out of spite more than need, she kept her boots on her feet. Her lace-up walking shoes weren't nearly as comfortable, but then, they'd come from the catalog company and hadn't been handmade to fit her perfectly. She chose a long, faded blue skirt from the clothing in the trunk and a snowy white shirtwaist with tiny little buttons from the high collar to the peplum waist. It would be filthy and dirt-stained by the end of the day, but right then she could have cared less. If Rafe Pierce wanted a prissy woman walking behind him, then she'd show him just how prissy and cold she could be.

"Oh, Mr. Rafe, thank you so much for saving my life out there. If you hadn't appeared on the scene I'm sure those savages would have scalped me," Connie said breathlessly just outside Willow's wagon.

"They weren't savages. They were civilized Indians and they wouldn't have scalped you, lady. And I hope you have learned a lesson. The reason we make a circle is to keep you all inside for safety. Don't go wandering out again," Rafe said gruffly.

"Yes, sir," Connie's voice dropped to a whisper and Willow could swear she was flirting with Rafe. "I'll stay close to you the rest of the way. That way I'll know I'm protected. I was so afraid while you were unconscious. I wanted to stay beside the river until you healed. I thought this whole idea of going on was foolish. But Willow Dulan will have her way and the rest of them voted with her."

"I see," Rafe said. "You better get on back to your chores and get ready for a long day of walking. Even if we have to stay at it until after dark, I intend to join the rest of the train before we stop."

"Yes, sir," Connie whispered, and Willow wanted to reach out there and slap some common sense into the girl.

Rafe breathed a heavy sigh of relief when Connie sashayed away, swaying her hips seductively. Whoever got that woman in Bryte better have a place so far out in the country that he only came to town once a year if he intended to keep her faithful. Rachel had been just like Connie, all blond and beautiful. Made Rafe's blood boil just watching her walk away from him like that. However, he'd learned that all that glittered was not necessarily gold. Sometimes it was iron pyrite. Fool's gold. That's what he'd gotten when he fell head over heels in love with Rachel. Just fool's gold. Pretty to look at. Pretty to hold. Yet more worthless than a handful of river sand.

An ant crawled across his bare foot, making him jump. His boots were in the wagon, where Willow was making enough noise stomping around that Hank and the rest of the wagon train could probably hear her all the way to the Mission. It didn't take a genius to know she was madder than a rattlesnake that'd been disturbed from a nice afternoon nap on a flat, warm rock. Just what set her off anyway? Sure, they'd had another argument, but he was right and she was wrong. If she was half the woman Katy was she'd realize that and admit it. Willow Dulan admit she was wrong? Now that was the silliest notion he'd come up with in his whole lifetime.

His head was throbbing and his bones were stiff from lying on the hard boards of the wagon floor for nigh onto twenty-four hours. A nasty fuzz coated the inside of his mouth and when he reached up to rub his jaw he found a quarter inch of dark bristle. His clothing was stiff from creek water and probably sweat, and he would have forsaken all twenty of the silly women for one nickel bath in a hotel and a professional barber's shave.

"Are you going to take all day in there?" He knocked

on the tailgate of the wagon. "I'd like to get cleaned up a bit myself."

"Well, pardon me." Willow threw back the wagon sheet with the finesse of an opera diva and ignored his raised hand to help her down. "I wouldn't want to keep the angel from his cloud. Don't bother saying thank you to any of us for all the work we've done or for saving your sorry, worthless hide either. Just get right on in there and clean up."

"Don't test me, Willow." His black eyes dared her to say another word.

"Don't tempt me, Rafe," she said just as coldly.

"Hey, Willow, come here and help me get this dumb ox harnessed up," Gypsy shouted. "He's more than I can handle."

"I'll be right there," Willow yelled back. "Harnessing dumb oxen is something I do quite well," she said, looking right at Rafe.

The sun beat down relentlessly on the sixteen women walking and the four driving in the middle of the afternoon. Rafe kept far enough of ahead of them that he couldn't hear their babbling and complaining, but he was sure the buzzing noise he heard behind him was just that. Twenty women. Four wagons. Sixteen oxen. Add that all together and it came up to one huge headache even if a man didn't have a bandage tied all the way around his head.

He'd pulled his extra suit of clothing from his saddlebags and found a wet washcloth in a basin of cold water. He'd taken off the stiff river-soaked garments that had dried to the form of his sleeping body. The soft, faded jeans felt good next to his semi-clean skin and the chambray shirt was nothing short of pure luxury when he buttoned it across his broad expanse of chest. Connie had been the first to reach his side when he stepped out of the back of the wagon. She carried a plate of hot bacon and several biscuits covered with redeye gravy. She'd fluttered her eyelashes and assured him that if he didn't eat, he'd surely faint along the way since he hadn't had a morsel of food in his mouth in two days. He ate the food and drank two cups of the bitter brew she called coffee, and ignored her constant prattle as he watched Willow expertly get her wagon ready for travel.

Lord, Almighty, he thought. *I bet she could have taken this whole train all the way to Bryte by herself. What she didn't know she'd learn along the way. But what man wants a woman like that? Doesn't she know men like women who need them? Need their masculine strength to protect them? I hope the man who gets her either has a strong will or else is a pure pansy and doesn't care that his wife will wear the britches in the family.*

When his stomach began to growl at midday he'd dropped back to find the women eating leftover biscuits from breakfast and not missing a single step. Gypsy was in the back of their wagon one minute, out the next with a greasy pillowcase full of biscuits filled with fried bacon. She passed one up to Gussie, who was driving that day, and handed out the rest to her other sisters. The rest of the women were doing the same. When Connie spied him, she yelled for him to come and claim one of their extra biscuits for his lunch.

"Thank you," he said as she handed him up four of the big round biscuits. "I'm beholden to you for remembering that your old scout needs nourishment."

"Oh, Mr. Rafe, I'll never forget your meals. You just come right on back to my wagon anytime. Me and Annie and the rest of us will be more than glad to take care of you," she said.

Willow swallowed a giggle. Poor, ignorant man was about to get into more trouble than he could crawl out of in a lifetime. Poor, stupid, young girl didn't know she was flirting with Beelzebub, not a real-life angel. She bit into her midday sandwich and looked out across the country-side. A few trees scattered around; an array of spring wildflowers that would make the most gorgeous bouquet. She visualized the blue bonnets, Black-eyed Susans, Indian paintbrush, buttercups, wild forget-me-nots, all in a crystal vase adorning the credenza in Aunt Nellie's foyer. There were no sights like this in downtown Mercersberg. There'd been wildflowers in the country when she'd lived with Aunt Harriet. But nothing to compare with miles and miles of rampant color dotting the minty green grass swaying in the midday breeze.

She wanted to take off her boots and walk barefoot for a couple of miles. Just to feel the soft grass on her feet. But just as sure as she did, she'd step on something and then Rafe Pierce would go into another rage. Just like Pete Hanson had done that last night she saw him.

"Whatever are you thinking about?" Gypsy asked. "One minute it looked like you were looking past the clouds and into the golden streets of Heaven. The next a shadow dropped down over your face and I could've sworn you saw a ghost."

"You read it pretty good," Willow said. "You reckon Connie will have him at the altar in a black suit before we get to Ash Hollow and get rid of him?"

"Nope, I don't. She's flirting but he's not biting. He's been burned before, I'd bet. Probably just like you. Besides, you said he was married to someone named Katy. Maybe we'd do well to tell her that. You know, if it wasn't for getting to know my sisters, I'd just about send off a message to my aunt and uncle in Texas from this Mission place we are headed for. I'd tell them to come and get me or send some money so I could come home. This is boring to walk all day. And this is only the second day of many. I don't like that Connie. She's too young to be on this trip."

"Oh, Gypsy, stay with us," Willow said. "What do you mean she's too young?"

"Fifteen," Gypsy whispered. "She told Annie she'd lied about her age to get to go. She's tall and pretty but mercy, fifteen?"

"She'll probably be sixteen before we get there and lots of women marry at that age, Gypsy. Us Dulans are really old maids already, you know. Every one of us could have already had a house full of kids. Connie just has a lot to learn, but she'll have her lessons down by the time we get to Bryte. Believe me, she'll be so tired of walking, she'll be ready for a home and a husband," Willow said.

"I might, too," Gypsy laughed.

"Well, I won't," Garnet said. "I'm just along for the trip. Hank better hope he keeps a hundred women alive to marry up with them men. Because this is one that ain't standing up there before the preacher man and promising to love, honor, and obey nothing that wears a pair of pants."

"Well, you obeyed Willow yesterday and she was wearing pants," Violet teased.

"Yes, but nobody made me promise to honor and love her," Garnet laughed easily.

Rafe figured they were discussing him and hoping he'd fall off his horse in a moaning heap beside the road. Well, he'd show all five of those Dulan witches. Tonight he'd take off the bandage and see for himself just how bad the cut had been. After he'd assessed the damage, then he'd go to Velvet Dulan like a gentleman and thank her for taking care of him, even if the idea did stick in his craw. He had no doubts she'd sewed him up and probably saved him from drowning when the horse tossed him in the snake-infested river. Willow would have let him drown or bleed to death. Then she would have danced a ring around his carcass. She was as witchy as Rachel had been.

And as strong as Katy. That's what draws you to her and you know it, his conscience chided. He ignored it as much as possible and scanned the horizon, looking for the mission.

Willow sank down deep into her own thoughts. Was it really fair to judge Rafe by Pete Hanson and his wicked ways? Probably not, but what else did she have to go by? Uncle Herman wasn't much better than Pete. Jake Dulan hadn't given her much of an example to raise her opinion of the male gender, either.

"Ghosts again?" Gypsy asked. "Want to talk about it?"

"No, talking about them just makes them more real. I need to bury them and get on with life," Willow said.

"Don't we all," said Gussie from the wagon seat.

Willow just nodded. It would be better when they joined the rest of the women. Once they were incorporated into the rest of the train, nothing could go wrong.

Chapter Seven

The earth ended in a flat line of dark green, and the sun, a perfect big round orange circle, dropped slowly toward that line. Willow imagined it falling into a pile of bright-colored mush when it hit the bottom. She was so entranced by the beauty before her that it took a while for her eyes to adjust and see what was between her and the Kansas sunset. It was the chuckle that brought her vision closer than the end of the world. Hank slapped his leg with his dusty hat and continued to laugh. Rafe just shook his head and sipped coffee from a blue granite cup at the camp he and the other men had made back away from the wagon train circle.

"Wonder what's so funny?" Garnet was close enough to Willow that it startled her.

"Probably getting a big kick out of the fact that the angel done got kicked off his pedestal and bent his halo," Willow said.

"I thought he'd fall off that horse by the time we got here," Garnet said. "He's a determined one, that Rafe Pierce. Probably just stayed tight in that saddle to prove you wrong."

"I don't care why he did it," Willow said. "But if he'd fallen off, I would have kept walking right past him. Dear little Connie could have taken care of him."

"Do I hear a little jealousy there, little sister?" Garnet raised an eyebrow, the corners of her mouth twitching as it held back a giggle.

"One has to like something before they can be jealous of it," Willow said shortly. "So do we get to go into the Mission tomorrow?"

"Changing the subject doesn't change the facts," Garnet said. "But, yes, I heard from the other ladies that tomorrow we'll be going to the Mission for one hour. That's all Hank allotted. Doesn't seem to be anything wrong with the wagons so we don't need a smithy. Haven't been on the road long enough to need too many supplies, but if there's something we want to purchase with our own money then we'll have a whole hour to buy it. Then we'll keep at it for an extra hour at the end of the day."

"Sounds fair enough, I suppose." Willow nodded.

"What sounds fair?" Velvet asked. "I came to round you two up for supper. I soaked beans all day and set them on to boil soon as we stopped. They're done. Used some of Willow's garlic to flavor them up and a little of the bacon."

"Sounds wonderful." Willow watched Rafe shake the grounds from the bottom of his cup and set it beside his saddle. He said something to the circle of men and Hank nodded seriously. Then he started toward the circle. Well, that's all she needed: Rafe Pierce joining all the women and Connie fussing over him. All Willow had heard since they'd joined the others an hour ago was Connie telling and retelling the story of how Rafe had come back from the dead and saved her from a whole band of roving wild Indians.

"Miss Velvet." Rafe stepped across the tongue of the wagon and ignored Willow altogether. "I've come to thank you for saving me from a watery grave and for stitching up the gash in my head. I took the bandage off and it's a fine sewing job. The scar should be faint when it's healed proper. Anyway, I want to thank you for taking care of me."

"What makes you think I did all that?" Velvet asked.

"You were at the back of the wagon. Willow was driving so she didn't see my horse toss me when he saw that snake. Had to have been you," he said.

"Well, you are wrong," Velvet said. "Willow came out of her clothing so fast we wondered how she did it. Then she dived right in the water and brought you up with her when she surfaced. She drug you to the shore with very little help from the rest of us. The ferryman only stayed long enough to see that you were alive and he left. Then Willow got out her medicine bag and sewed you up. She even rode your horse and scouted the way for us, and insisted our wagon be first in line so it would be closer if you needed her for anything. So it's her you should be thanking, not me."

Rafe's jaws worked in clenched rage. He'd rather have drowned than have to thank Willow Dulan for anything. She was nothing short of a festered splinter in the bottom of his foot. Every step just brought more pain and agitation.

"Don't bother," Willow said. "I wouldn't let a mangy dog die if I could help him. Not that you're on the same level as a cur mutt. I'd enjoy saving a helpless dog. Good night, Rafe." She flipped around and walked away from him and her two sisters.

"She's a . . ." He couldn't find the right word to call the woman.

"Be careful. She's our sister." Garnet's blue eyes flashed. "And blood is thicker than water, cowboy. You say anything mean about her behind her back and we'll be obliged to take up for her. You got anything you want to say to her face, then it's for her and you to settle it and we won't step in, but don't you mutter a bad word against her to us when she can't hear it. Understand?"

Rafe glowered at Garnet but she didn't back down from the heat of his anger. "The bunch of you better stay out of my way. I told Hank he'd be sorry he brought you, and I was right."

"Oh, honey," Velvet said, "you better not be sorry Hank let us come along for the trip. If he hadn't, you'd be six feet under right now. You don't have to worry about us staying out of your way. We won't bother you, Rafe Pierce. We're Dulans and we're sisters and we take up for our own, and there ain't a one of us that wants a thing to do with a married man. So you stay out of our way and we'll stay out of yours. But if I was you, I'd sure set Connie straight. She needs to know that you are married."

Rafe's mind was reeling. Married? Him? Where did they get that notion? And where did they get the idea there was anything between him and Connie? He might be drawn to yellow-haired beauties, but not someone as young as Connie. She was so young, she still thought she could flutter her eyelashes and lower her voice and grown men would melt in puddles at her toes.

"Good night, ladies," Rafe finally said and disappeared into the dusk, back to the men's camp to try to sort out what Velvet and Garnet had said. So the sassy Willow had been the one who took care of him. That was probably the reason he kept talking about Rachel in his sleep, because they were surely alike in more ways than one. When he roused up and saw her in the wagon, it was only natural he would mistake her for Rachel. Willow was by far the more beautiful of the two women, but then Rachel could make any red-blooded man's eyes pop right out of his head. In comparison, Willow was a little more rough around the edges than Rachel, who'd been polished to a fine sheen. Actresses should be polished that well, though, and she was a good actress, both on stage and off. She'd used her talent and brought Rafe Pierce to his knees in only a few weeks. He shook his head in confusion and refilled his coffee cup. He pretended to listen to the conversation the boys were having concerning the next day's journey, but his mind kept wandering back to that first time he'd laid eyes on the famous Rachel Throckmorton. She'd been on the stage in

Lincoln, singing with the sweetest soprano voice to ever float over his head.

After the show, he and the friends he was visiting attended a reception in a fancy hotel lobby and Rachel made an appearance. He could scarcely believe his good fortune when she singled him out from all the men there. A few weeks later he proposed and she accepted. They would be married as soon as the play finished its engagement. She'd come to southern Nebraska and they'd be married on his ranch. His older sister, Katy, would take care of the reception for all the neighbors and friends.

"Rafe?" Hank said. No answer. "Rafe?" He raised his voice a little. "Rafe!" He finally yelled.

"Yes?" Rafe looked around in bewilderment. "Did you say something?"

"Yes, I did. While you were staring into the fire like you were watching a chorus line of fancy women on a stage or something," Hank said. "Are you sure your head is all right, son? You think you can make it all the way to Ash Hollow?"

"Just had my mind on the past. Now what did you ask?" Rafe raised an eyebrow and pain shot through the wound on his forehead. "Ouch!" he exclaimed.

"Hurts, don't it?" Hank grinned. "But that Velvet sure sewed it up pretty. Never did see such little bitty stitches on something as sorry as your old hide. If I get cut open on this trip just take me to her and she can fix me up."

"Velvet didn't do it. Willow did," Rafe said bluntly.

"Who?" Bobby guffawed. "I thought you said she was the one who put on overalls and boots and played wagon master all day. Is she that tall, plain one with the bun at the back of her head? The one that looks at us menfolks like we're something she got on her feet out at the hog lot?"

"No, Willow is the one with the blond curly hair. The short one with the white blouse and the dark blue skirt," Rafe said.

"You mean that beautiful one? The one in the last wagon?" Bobby asked, amazed.

"That's the one, but remember, Bobby: Just because it glitters don't mean it's gold," Rafe said.

Hank grinned. "Well, she said she could do anything. I suppose she wasn't just blowing smoke up my nose, was she?"

"I guess not," Rafe ceded. "I'm going to sleep. Going to be a long day tomorrow. What was it you asked me?"

"Done forgot while we were talking about them stitches on your head," Hank said. "Suppose we'd all better turn in. I'll make a round through the circle and see that everything is winding down. We'll have an hour at the Mission tomorrow and then cross the bridge over Wolf Creek. Hope to get a full ten miles in tomorrow even with the hour at the Mission. In a week they'll be seasoned up and we'll start getting fifteen a day on good flat land. When we hit the hills, it'll slow us down, but I still think we can get there before the snow."

Rafe nodded but didn't answer. He used his saddle for a pillow and shut his eyes but it was a long time before he went to sleep. Somehow Rachel, Willow, Katy and even Garnet kept haunting his thoughts and interfering with his sleep.

Willow claimed a section of ground under the wagon and stretched out for the night. That Rafe Pierce was a rogue. A selfish rogue and not a lot better than Pete Hanson— who held the title for being the world's worst rascal. She shut her eyes tightly to erase the vision of Pete: tall, blond-haired, green eyes. So handsome he'd taken her breath away the first time she saw him in church. No matter how tight she squeezed her eyelids, he was still there, in his fine three-piece suits and perfect hair.

There was no way he'd even see someone like me, she remembered thinking back on that Sunday morning when Pete showed up in the pew right in front of her and Aunt

Harriet. After services, all the eligible females began flirting, which was something Willow didn't even know how to do. She and Aunt Harriet could do the work of four men on the farm. She'd been trained when to work the cattle, when to plant corn and beans, how to keep books to show their profits and losses. But feminine flirting wasn't within the realm of her abilities, and she felt strangely inadequate as she admired the gorgeous Peter Hanson.

When he had come calling that afternoon, she'd almost swooned, and Aunt Harriet had laughed. Two weeks later Aunt Harriet was dead. Willow moved into town with her Aunt Nellie and Uncle Herman. Six weeks later Pete proposed and Willow didn't even hesitate when she said "yes." For a month she was the happiest woman in all of Mercersberg, Pennsylvania. Then it fell apart. One minute she was looking at white satin for a bridal gown and planning a church wedding. The next she was on a stagecoach coming home from Luray, Virginia, with nothing but a broken heart and the determination never to trust another man. When she reached Mercersberg, there was the letter from Hank and the ticket to St. Joseph, Missouri.

Pete had shown up just moments before she boarded the coach. He said that he just came to give her one chance to come to her senses. He still needed a respectable wife to give him sons to run the plantation he would soon inherit. No, he was not sorry for his little tryst, and never would be. Lucy would always be a part of his life, but he'd keep it discreet and never make a fool of Willow in public. She would have his money, his legitimate children, and a place in society.

"But what about your heart, Pete? Isn't that what I'm supposed to have when I'm your wife?" she'd asked him bluntly as they had loaded her trunk on the top of the stagecoach.

"My heart will always belong to Lucy. It has since we were sixteen. But I'll be a good husband to you," he had said gruffly.

Willow opened her eyes and stared up at the bottom of the wagon. There were no tears streaming down her cheeks. Those had come on the trip from Luray back to Mercersberg on a cold spring night. She'd cried until there were no more tears, then she'd cried some more. She'd been a complete fool to trust Pete.

It had been a horrible lesson. *What was it Aunt Harriet had said? Burn me once, shame on you. Burn me twice, shame on me. Well, I got scalded pretty good, and they'll sell ice-cold mint julips inside the gates of Hades before I let myself in for another heartache like that.*

She finally went to sleep, only to dream of Pete Hanson, who kept falling into the river and she had to rescue him. Something in her heart wanted to let him drown, but she couldn't. Viciously cruel though he had been, she couldn't watch him die in that murky water. No sooner than she'd get him hauled up to the shore than he'd get on his horse, ride back out into the water, and fall off again. By the time she awoke she was even more tired than she'd been the night before.

"Thirty minutes, ladies." Rafe made the circle, letting them know it was time to get down to the business of closing the gap between them and the husband material waiting on the other end.

Willow glared at him over the top of her coffee mug, but she didn't say anything. From where she sat the cut on his head looked like it was mending just fine. He swaggered around the circle like a proud young lion, so evidently the concussion, if he had had one, had taken care of itself. She tossed back the last swallow of lukewarm coffee but didn't taste the bitter brew. The honesty at the inner grain of her being made her admit to herself that she found Rafe Pierce attractive. But then, she'd found Pete handsome, too, and felt drawn to him. Just look at the garden path that little adventure had led her down. No, she'd be honest and admit those brown eyes were mesmerizing and the way he filled out his jeans, like Gypsy had said, was very appealing. But even if he was available, Willow still didn't know how to flirt, and she sure didn't mess around with married men.

Willow hopped up on the seat of the wagon and slapped the reins against the four oxen. Four big brown beasts of burden with no thoughts except to walk until they were told to stop and then eat the plentiful grass until it was time to be harnessed up again. *Too bad*, Willow thought, *that human beings can't function the same way. Why did God give us a heart anyway? Seems like it's always hurting for something. Either something you can have and don't want, or something you can't have and do want. Doesn't make a bit of sense.*

"So did you see that Bobby fellow? Cute little thing, ain't he?" Annie asked Connie right beside Willow's wagon.

"Oh, he's just a baby. Now you want to set eyes upon a real man, you look at that Rafe Pierce. He's the handsome one among those menfolks," Connie replied.

"Well, honey, you'd best keep your eyes forward and not be drinking in the sight of that cowboy," Gypsy informed her. "While he was out like a light in the back of our wagon, we found out he's married to someone named Katy."

"Well, he didn't tell me that and—" Connie broke off, blushing to the roots of her blond hair.

"And what? Did he make any advances toward you?" Annie asked.

"No, he's been the perfect gentleman, but if he was married, he would have told me. I just know it. I can tell by the way he looks at me when . . ." She left the sentence hanging in the air.

"Connie, don't be a fool," Willow said from the wagon seat. "Married men don't always go around bragging up their wives, especially when some young girl is flitting around them like a bee on clover."

"Don't you talk to me like that." Connie shot daggers toward Willow.

"Hey, I'm just trying to help." Willow shook her head. Lord, if she had a choice she'd gladly walk. The seat of the wagon got harder every minute.

"You probably just made that up so you can have him," Connie accused.

Willow smiled. "I don't want him."

"Hey, girl, you better remember that you signed on to go to Bryte to marry some gold miner there. Someone who's promised to have you a house ready to move into and will be a good husband to you," Annie reminded Connie.

"Why walk all that way and marry someone you don't even know when you could have someone right now and get it over with?" Connie said.

"Then you better look at Bobby," Gypsy said. "He's probably a couple or three years older than you and he's not married already."

"But he's part Indian," Connie said just above a whisper.

"That a problem?" Gypsy narrowed her eyes.

"I didn't mean no harm. It's plain you're part Indian too. Why don't you make a try for Bobby?" Connie shot back at her.

"I am not part Indian, lady. I'm half Dulan and the other half is pure Mexican. No Indian here, and Bobby just ain't my type. I'm going to California and marry a tall Swede. One with blond hair and eyes the color of a summer sky. Then for the rest of my life I'm going to make him feel like a god," Gypsy said.

"Good luck," Connie smarted off and picked up her pace until she was walking with the women three wagons ahead.

They reached the Mission an hour earlier than Hank had predicted and left the wagons in a straight line beside the building. Willow was amazed for the second time at the size of this brick building in the middle of the United States. She'd read about this part of the world but never in her wildest imagination would she have pictured something as elegant as the Patee House or something as big as the Indian Mission right out there in the corner of Missouri.

"It's fifty-two feet high, one hundred and seven feet long and thirty-seven feet wide," Rafe said, reading her mind so well that it baffled her.

"Thank you for that information," she said coldly.

"It was meant to house far more Indians than it does. Cholera and smallpox killed them off not long after it was built. The missionaries teach spelling, arithmetic, and geography," he said, keeping step beside her, leading his horse.

"I see," she said, frowning at Gypsy, who had turned back to grin at her.

"I'll be getting along now," he said. "Just noticed the amazement in your eyes when you saw the building. And Willow—"

"Hey, yoo-hoo, Rafe." Connie waved and came running back to him. "Where would I find an extra coffee cup at this fort? We only have five in our gear and there might be a time we'd like to have a little company."

"I suppose you'd get it at the general store in there." Rafe nodded toward one of the outbuildings.

"Would you walk with me and show me where it is?" She batted her lashes at him.

"Sorry, ma'am, I've got to play guard and stay with the wagons. You go on and I'm sure the preacher's wife will be glad to help you, but don't be spending your money on a cup. You invite someone to supper or coffee and they can bring their own cup. I think everyone has one of their own on the train. 'Course, if you're thinking of company from somewhere else?" He tried to keep the bitterness from his voice. He was going to apologize to Willow for not thanking her the night before, and now the moment was gone. Willow had used the time Connie wasted to go on ahead with her sisters.

"Of course not," Connie giggled. "Thank you so much for the idea. Of course, you'll have to bring your own cup and plate, too, when we invite you to supper at our little campsite."

Rafe mounted his horse and looked down at the girl. "We can't do that, Miss. Our contract says we won't encourage any of that kind of thing with the ladies on this train. You have a contract to marry a man at the end of the journey, and we have one that says we'll get you there respected and respectable."

"We'll just see about that." Connie laughed as he rode away.

Indians of all ages and sizes came out of the Mission and watched the ladies make their way across the open field. Bobby, half Iowa Indian himself, entertained them with the story of three of his relatives who had come upon the sleeping Connie and scared her so badly. The children wanted to know right away which woman was Connie, and then they wanted to know which one was Willow, the brave woman who'd been wagon master for a day. Willow sounded like an Indian name to them and they ran to her when Bobby pointed her out.

"Come and sit with us," said one young girl with long black braids and eyes as dark as a lump of coal. "Tell us about the big snake you kept from killing our Rafe."

"*Your* Rafe?" Willow asked, as several of them pulled her to the shade of a tree.

"Yes, he has come here five or six times," a teenage boy said. "He stops as he takes the trains to Ash Hollow and he stops when he goes to St. Joe to get them. We all love Rafe. He brings us candy and tells us stories. Where is he? He isn't really dead, is he?"

"No, he'll probably be along in a little while. He's taking care of business at the wagon train," she said surprised at their devotion.

Kids of all ages sat down around her, eyes eager for a story, ears ready to listen, and minds ready for something other than the monotony of lessons and hard work. Gypsy winked at her from the sidelines and waved as she joined the other sisters in a trip to the general store. Willow almost begged off but she couldn't disappoint the children.

"I came a long way to St. Joe to see my father, but he was already dead when I got there," she started. If they wanted a story, she'd tell them one that would last the full hour and make it a history lesson at the same time. She told them about Mercersberg, a whole month by stagecoach, to the east. The history of the town that was already near a hundred years old, and the mountains she'd crossed. The fear in her heart that the stage would crash down the side, and the constant bouncing, like a boat on dry land.

By the time the hour was up, she'd told them about the big, vicious snake who scared their Rafe's horse and made it buck him off into the water. She gave the snake a voice and made it tell the story of the huge monster horse with another monster attached to its back. How the snake had to think fast and mesmerize the horse with its evil eyes so that the horse would be frightened of it. Then how the snake searched in the water for the second monster so it could sting him with his fangs, but Willow pulled him to the banks of the river just in time to thwart the snake's plans.

She had no idea that Rafe and the Presbyterian minister who took care of the mission were listening from behind the edge of an outbuilding. She was remembering the few times the peddler had come by their ranch and told her stories when she was a little girl. Aunt Harriet told her later they were just a bunch of lies he made up on the spot, but Willow didn't care. They'd entertained her, and she hoped she'd done the same for the Indian children.

"Ohhhh," one of the smaller girls sighed when Willow stopped talking.

Willow noticed most of the women were already back at their wagons. "Well, that's all I can tell you for now. We've got to move on, and it's my turn to drive the wagon today."

"Thank you, Miss Willow. Could we . . ." the older girl

stammered. "It's just that I think you might be Indian somehow. I think you are a descendent of the storytellers. Would you stay here with us?"

"I'd second that." The minister stepped up in the middle of the children. "I knew Jake Dulan and I don't know if he had a bit of Indian in him. With all that blond hair and Dulan eyes, I wouldn't want to say that you've got an ounce of true Indian blood. But you sure can weave a story. I listened behind the building there. We got a printing press a few years ago and we've used it mainly to make grammar books and hymnals for the children. But I've got an idea you could do well writing stories for them. I bet I could get Hank to release you from the bride contract."

Willow smiled so beautifully that for a moment Rafe thought she'd take the reverend up on his offer. Her eyes sparkled and a dimple deepened in her left cheek. "No, thank you for the offer, but no. I've got four sisters out there I'm just getting to know. I'll need to go with them."

Rafe let out the air that he didn't even know he was holding in his lungs. If the children hadn't begun to clamor, he was sure he would have given his hiding place away. All of them wanted to touch her hand or her yellow hair or just wrap their arms around her waist and hug her. Total acceptance of a total stranger. Something so foreign to the Indian culture and so strange to watch from his vantage point.

"Well, then let me pay you for the story. Usually we charge the wagons twenty-five cents each to cross our toll bridge over Wolf Creek. Sometimes if they're really big wagons we charge fifty cents. So today to pay for this wonderful hour you've spent with our children, we won't charge you anything. I'll let Hank know that he crosses for free today. And Willow Dulan, anytime you change your mind, there's a place at the Iowa Sac and Fox Mission waiting for you." The reverend extended his hand and they shook.

"Good-bye, Willow Storyteller." The children all

waved as she hurried back to her wagon, her heart lighter than it had been in months.

"So, Rafe Pierce, you can come out now," the teenage boy said just above a whisper. "Are you really going to let that storyteller get away from you?"

"That storyteller is a witch," Rafe growled, but he couldn't keep the grin from his handsome face.

"All storytellers are witches. They've lived more than one life and seen more things than the rest of us," the boy said. "You better wake up, Rafe."

"Sage advice from a kid," Rafe chuckled.

"An Indian kid." The boy slapped Rafe on the arm. "Indian kids see more than you white eyes do. When will we see you again?"

"Not for a while. This is Hank's last trip. If you are ever in Ash Hollow, go north and come see me." Rafe waved at the boy as he mounted his horse and rode back to the wagons.

Willow watched him from the wagon seat and wondered what the teenage boy was saying. Was he joking with him about the snake that had a human voice? Whatever they were talking about didn't matter, because Rafe Pierce was only along for the first leg of the journey and then she'd never see him again.

Besides, he was married.

Chapter Eight

Soft spring breezes continued to blow through the campsite at the end of the day, making Willow as restless as the wind. The whole area had looked like a Chicago laundry house earlier, with ropes strung from every available wagon corner, tree, or whatever the ladies could find to hold clotheslines. Hank had given them half a day to rest after a week of travel, and he'd stopped right beside the most beautiful creek they'd seen since leaving Missouri. It didn't take them long to gather up their laundry and soap and set about doing the washing. When that was finished, they went in groups of five or ten to the rapidly flowing little creek and bathed, washing the clothing they wore before they returned to the campsite.

Willow's soft nightgown smelled fresh from the breeze that had cooperated with them all day, drying their clothing and bedding quickly. The odor of the rose-scented soap she'd shared with her sisters still clung to her skin. Tomorrow night they wouldn't have a creek, and she'd have to make do with a basin bath. But tonight she hummed as she pulled her shawl around her shoulders, expecting the gesture to put an end to the restlessness in her soul. It didn't. There was a struggle there: one part wanting something it couldn't even describe, the other being content with a perfect day.

If she could watch the sunset and listen to the bubbling creek at the same time, it might put an end to the itch down deep in her soul. She braided her hair into one long rope that hung down her back and pictured the little creek going about its merry way, flowing over the rocks. Sure, Hank had made the rule about not going outside the camp without a partner. But that was for skittish women like Connie, not bullheaded, stubborn, and independent Willow Dulan. She wrapped her shawl tightly around her shoulders and started toward the tongue of the wagon, which was laid against the backside of Connie and Annie's wagon.

"Did you hear something?" Willow heard Connie ask Annie inside the wagon.

"No, and you didn't either. You've got to be the most wary girl I've ever known," Annie said.

"Well, if you'd almost had your hair removed by a bunch of renegade Indians, you'd be wary, too," Connie snapped.

Willow smiled and watched her step more closely, tiptoeing until she was well out of hearing distance. She hummed as she made her way to the edge of the creek. The place where they'd washed clothing and bathed lay in a copse of trees so thick she couldn't see the sunset after all. Disappointed, but only for a moment, she sighed in defeat. Then she saw a rise just up the creek where she could sit and watch the sunset and hear the flow of the water at the same time.

Rafe waited until all the women had had their time in Clear Creek. Then he waited while Hank and the other hired hands took their turn. He didn't mind being last because he wanted his bath to be the last thing he did before he turned in. One night in a clean bed with a clean body would ensure him a good night's rest; he was positive. That was something he hadn't had in a whole week. Every night he dreamed of Rachel or Willow Dulan or both. And every time Rachel fired that gun, he awoke in a sweat worse than the one he worked up through the day. He was sure that one night of fresh-smelling clothing and bedding would make the difference.

He loved the feel of the cool water against his skin, and the lye soap wasn't harsh. Katy was proud of her soap-making abilities. Sometimes she put scent in it, but not in the cakes she'd given him for the trip. It was just plain old clean-smelling soap. He lathered his body and lay back in the rushing waters, letting the bubbles rinse away. This was almost as good as a long soak in a tub in his ranch house, he thought. But it couldn't hold a light to that little water-fall on the back side of his property. There the creek came over the top of a rock formation and fell into a small deep pool that eventually flowed on into the great Nemaha River. *Now that was a real bath*, he thought as he shampooed his black hair and the week-old beard he planned to shave in a few minutes.

With a long sigh, he crawled up out of the water and sat on the grassy knoll, letting the breeze dry his wet skin and hair. After a few minutes, he reached for his clean jeans and slipped them on, letting the suspenders fall to the sides. He took his granite cup to the edge of the creek and dipped some water in on top of another piece of soap, this one with a faint scent of pine. He picked up a piece of broken mirror no bigger than the palm of his hand and set it in the fork of a scrub oak tree. He hung the razor strop over a limb and swiped his straight razor across it several times until it had a fine-honed edge. He used a small brush to work up a lather in the cup and then painted his face with it.

Just as he raised the razor to his face, he caught a glimpse of a movement in the mirror. His face full of lather, his guns at least ten yards away, and nothing but a razor for a weapon, he whipped around to see just what or who was sneaking up on him. "What are you doing here?" he asked gruffly when he realized just who was disturbing him.

Willow jumped like she'd been hit by a bolt of lightning.

"I might ask you the same thing," she smarted right back at him. So much for a wonderful ending to a perfect day.

"I'm having my bath. Waited until you all were finished. So go away," Rafe said. What must he look like, standing there with the upper half of his body uncovered and his face all white with soap? Besides, the sun was fading fast and if he didn't shave, he'd lose the light to do it by.

"I'm going to watch the sunset and listen to the water," Willow said bluntly. "I'll turn my back and ignore you, but don't say a word, because I don't want my quiet time spoiled." Her voice had an icy edge and the words sounded real enough, but Willow knew they were a hundred and ten percent bluff. There was no way she'd have a quiet time with Rafe Pierce standing behind her looking like that.

"Fine!" he exclaimed and went back to his task. He could see the top of her yellow hair at the bottom of his mirror. Why, oh why, did he have to be attracted to women with light-colored hair? After Rachel, anybody would think he'd never want to look at another pretty woman with blond hair. Katy said he needed a plain, overweight woman with a good disposition. Not so pretty that she'd think she was above him. Not built so well he'd have to fight every man around. A good disposition and the ability to keep his home and hearth clean and get the meals on the table for him.

"Ouch," he muttered when he nicked the slight cleft in his chin. Blood bubbled up but he ignored it. There would be time later to dot it with a little alum if it didn't stop on its own. Right now the sun was setting fast and he had to finish the job or there'd be lots of nicks on his face.

Rafe dabbed at the blood and scraped the last of the beard away. Willow was still there, and his conscience pricked him. He'd had a whole week and there had been plenty of opportunities to thank her for saving him and stitching his head. But every time he started to say something, Connie interrupted or else his tongue was suddenly glued to the roof of his mouth and he couldn't utter a word. He leaned forward and checked his forehead where the stitches had been. She'd taken them out just last night without a word, just smooth fingers brushing across his skin as she removed the black thread without causing him one bit of pain. He'd walked away without thanking her for that either. Katy would have his hide tacked to the smokehouse door for his rudeness.

Before she turned away from Rafe, Willow noticed the long scar across the top of his back, running from one shoulder to the other. As she sat there, doing her best to ignore Rafe Pierce, she wondered if that was where they'd surgically removed his big, fluffy wings. She heard him utter the single word "ouch" and practically jumped to her feet to rush to his side, but held herself in check. If he'd cut his throat and was bleeding to death, she'd hear him flopping around like a fish out of water. She'd have enough time to save him . . . maybe.

She felt his presence and breathed in the fresh aroma of pine-scented soap, but she didn't take her eyes from the sunset. He'd still be sitting there at the second coming for all she cared. He was the most aggravating man she'd ever dealt with. Not that she'd had occasion to deal with that many. Just Pete Hanson, Uncle Herman, and a few young swans who'd tried to come courting her in her early teens.

"Willow, I want to thank you for saving my life, stitching me up, and taking out the stitches," he said, all in a rush, knowing that if he didn't get it all out at once, something would surely disturb them. He surely did hope it wasn't that chatterbox Connie. Lord, all he needed was for Connie to catch them together: Willow in her nightrail and a shawl and him without a shirt on. Hank would have a pure hissy fit, and the women would shun Willow.

"You are welcome," she said, without revealing any of the breathless emotion that was stirring her heart into a mass of mush.

"Lovely sunset," he said.

"Yes, it is." Willow nodded, catching a glimpse of a chest full of dark hair in her peripheral vision. A chill inched its way up her backbone and she pulled the shawl closer to her body, but the frigid feeling was too deep for a mere flannel scrap of material to reach.

"Most beautiful I've ever seen," he whispered, so close to her ear that she could feel the warmth of his breath on her neck. That sent another cold burst through her body. Pete Hanson had never affected her like that.

She turned to say something and got lost in his gaze. One moment she was sinking into the depths of pecan-colored eyes and the next his lips were on hers, sending fireworks exploding through her brain. Bells rang. Her heart sang. Her arms went around his neck and the shawl dropped on the green grass. She tasted a mixture of creek water, pine-scented soap, and alcohol. *So that's what kisses are supposed to be like*, she thought dreamily when his tongue skimmed her lower lip.

He's married, her conscience reminded her somewhere in the middle of the ecstasy. She drew back from him with a jerk and slapped fire into his cheek at the same time.

"What's that for? You were enjoying that as much as I was," Rafe said, rubbing his face and wondering if the woman might be touched in the head.

"Go tell Katy that," Willow said bluntly, gathering her shawl back around her shoulders and standing up. "Maybe she'll even sew your wings back on for you."

"What are you talking about? Why would I tell Katy I kissed a woman?" he asked, his brows drawn down in question.

"I guess you *would* have trouble telling your wife, who probably thinks you are some kind of real angel, that you kissed another woman. Well, I can sure enough tell you from experience, Mr. Pierce—even though I wasn't a full-fledged wife—women don't take too kindly to their intended kissing on other women. I can just imagine how a real wife would feel. So that's what that was for," she said.

Mercy, but she was lovely, standing there with a long braid down her back and a faded shawl around her shoulders. And bare feet. She looked more like an angel than anything he'd ever seen. "Katy is not my wife," Rafe said. "Sit back down. I'll tell you about Katy. Guess I owe you that much since I mumbled on and on about her and Rachel while I was out cold."

"You don't owe me anything," Willow said.

"Please." Rafe reached out and took her hand in his.

Tingles of shock dashed up her arms and shot through her soul. Her feet were glued to the grass and pure magic couldn't have made her walk away from him and his pleading eyes. She sat down, withdrew her quivering hand from his, and tucked it inside her shawl.

"I was engaged to Rachel Throckmorton," he said in a faraway voice.

"*The* Rachel Throckmorton? The actress and singer?" Willow asked, amazed.

"That's the one. I met her in Lincoln five years ago. I was twenty years old and she was a couple of years older. I proposed and she accepted. We were to be married on my ranch when she finished her engagement there. I was a fool thinking she could ever come to a Nebraska ranch and be happy. Anyway, the engagement ended and she came to my ranch. She . . ." He cleared his throat and looked out over the dark forms of the trees in the distance to where the last of the sun's rays were disappearing and dusk was bringing on the night.

"Hey, Rafe, you don't owe me an explanation or your life story." She wanted to touch his face, his arm, even hug him and tell him everything was fine. The pain in his voice cut through her like a two-edged fillet knife.

"She and my sister, Katy, didn't like each other from the first day. Katy's eight years older than me and has six kids. She married the rancher right next door so our places adjoin each other. Anyway, I figured Rachel would come to love Katy and her brood of kids as much as I do. Just give her lots of time, and we had that ahead of us. A whole future full of time. It was the night before the wedding. I'd been staying at Katy's at night and letting Rachel have my house. Keeping things right proper, you know. Anyway, I'd forgotten my dress boots. I needed them to go with the suit I was wearing to the wedding the next day, so I just saddled up Buster and rode over to the house to get them. The house was just around the bend and I noticed a buggy sitting in the front yard. I didn't recognize it, but it didn't bother me much until I saw Rachel and a man walking from the barn to the house. They were all hugged up together, so I just edged Buster back up under a shade tree and waited until they went in the house."

Willow had lived this story in a different state with little variation. She could have finished it for him, but she sat still and waited while he collected his thoughts. Maybe talking about it would exorcise it from his mind. Perhaps that's what she needed to do. Talk to Gypsy or one of her other sisters about that time in her life when she'd trusted Pete Hanson.

"I opened the door very quietly fifteen minutes later and could hear them in the bedroom. She was telling him not to worry. As soon as we were married she'd take care of the matter and sell the ranch. The two of them should have enough money to build their own theater with what she'd get out of it. Being my wife for a week or two was a small price to pay for a long future together, she assured him. He asked her how she intended to take care of the problem, and she said with arsenic. It had worked on her first two husbands and no one had suspected a thing."

"Oh, my," Willow gasped. At least Peter hadn't intended to kill her. Or had he? Once she had him the legitimate heirs he wanted so badly, would he have removed her from the scene? That way he'd have Lucy and heirs both.

"I slung open the door to find her laid up in what was going to be our marriage bed and the man half dressed, just standing there with this big grin on his face. He said, 'So we meet, Rafe Pierce. I suppose it's a little early and goodness knows this will change our plans.' Real quiet-like and confident."

"What did you do?" she asked.

"I didn't have time to do anything. Rachel grabbed a gun from the little table beside the bed and aimed it right at me," Rafe said. "She laughed and said that since I'd already fixed the will to leave her everything in the case of my death, that she didn't care if we were married or not. If I was dead, she didn't have to pretend to love me for a week, and I could just die with a bullet in the heart instead of rat poison in the stomach. She cocked the pistol and I could tell by the look in her eyes that she meant what she said. I told her Katy would burn her at the stake and she just laughed. I dived for the floor when the pistol went off and hit my head on the bedpost on the way down. The bullet grazed my back but there was a lot of blood and I was out cold so they figured they'd done the job. Next thing I knew Katy and Rachel were both in the room with me. Rachel was wringing her hands and telling some story about finding me on the floor like that and hurrying to Katy's house to get help. She moaned something about how she could never live without me, and that's when I opened my eyes."

"Bet that really thwarted her plans," Willow said.

"Sure did. I told Katy to get rid of her. I wouldn't press charges. But I wanted the sheriff to know about her past two husbands. The next morning when I woke up, Katy had me bandaged up and Rachel was gone. Felt pretty stupid for a while, especially when the neighbors and friends told me that I should've been smart enough to know I couldn't keep a songbird on a Nebraska ranch," he said.

"So you're not married and never have been?" Willow asked.

"Nope, and don't intend to be. I'll just enjoy Katy's kids and leave my ranch to the oldest boy when I'm dead and gone. Don't know that I'd ever trust another woman," he said.

"Then I apologize for the slap. But don't ever kiss me

again, Rafe Pierce. Because I've got a story very similar to yours in my past and I don't intend to marry either. I could never trust another man. And I don't want to be led down the garden path with a few kisses," she told him.

"Want to tell me your story?" he asked.

"His name was Pete Hanson. He owned a plantation. He proposed to me. I accepted. Went to the plantation to meet his folks and like you, was in a place where I wasn't supposed to be one evening. Found out the love of his life was a squatter's daughter that his parents would never accept for a daughter-in-law and mother of their grandchildren. He and Lucy had a son already and I heard him promise her that once he had a legitimate heir to satisfy his father, our marriage would be "in name only." I left the plantation and came back to Mercersberg, where I found the letter had arrived from Hank, along with the tickets and the reservations. Pete came to the stage station and told me he'd make me a good husband and give me a good name but his heart would always belong to Lucy. I left. You know the rest."

Few words, Lots of pain. Rafe could hear it and feel it. The scars on his heart were five years old. The ones on hers were still fresh.

"I'm sorry," he said gently.

"Don't be. Like you, I was pretty stupid. Should've realized Pete Hanson wasn't interested in a plain old country girl like me. Now I'm going back to camp. You reckon you could wait a couple of minutes before you show up? Somehow, I don't reckon it would set too well with the rest of them to know that I've been sitting out here with you," she said.

"Friends?" Rafe stuck out his hand.

"Friends." Willow nodded and shook his hand firmly. The touch of his callused hand surrounding hers sent a red hot heat all the way to her face. She turned and briskly walked back to the campsite without looking back. There was nothing there, not even if his touch made her knees weak. Not even if he had kissed her and the world lit up in a bright array of gorgeous colors.

"Hey, what'd you mean you weren't getting married, ever? Isn't that why you are on this wagon train?" Rafe called out softly.

"There will be a hundred women alive when we get there. If I have to nurse them all back from their deathbeds, there'll be a hundred. None of them are going to die," she vowed. But she didn't look back.

"Plain old country girl," he muttered. "Sorry, Willow Dulan. That's something you'll never be."

Chapter Nine

Willow trudged along beside the wagon, grateful that she'd been used to hard work her whole life. Some of the women complained of leg cramps at night after the long, long hours of walking every day. But so far, Willow had had more trouble with boredom than with physical pain. Rafe had avoided her like she had the pox ever since that night when he told her about Rachel. That was fine, too. Her heart wouldn't hold up to very many of his kisses. She wondered, though, if the man she married in California would be able to rattle her senses like Rafe had done when his tongue brushed against her lower lip.

"So what are you thinking about now?" Gypsy asked. "Don't ever hear you fussing about the journey, or the lack of hot baths, or the food. A body would think you are actually enjoying this trip."

"Sure I am," Willow smiled. "I'm finding out that Gussie is mostly growl and not a lot of bite."

"I heard that," Gussie said from the wagon seat. "And honey, I might be mostly bluff, but let me tell you something—when I bite something, it better be dropping down on its knees and making peace with St. Peter because it's going to be visiting with him right soon."

Willow laughed. "I wouldn't doubt it, Gussie. And I've

found out that you, Gypsy, are not a fragile little woman with no backbone."

Gypsy nodded, a sweet smile creating dimples on her cheeks. "That's right. I might not bite like Gussie, but I can sure use a pistol and keep vile people in line."

"Velvet is just like her name. Soft and gentle, but underneath she's got a core of steel. She might not know it yet, but she could probably outfight any one of us," Willow said.

"I don't think so." Velvet pushed a wisp of straggling brown hair back away from her forehead where it had stuck in her sweat. "I'd love to have your spunk, Willow. Every time I have to face a confrontation, I just back down."

"You've got the spunk, Velvet, and you'll use it when the time comes. It's there beneath all that pretty soft outside shell. Believe me, the Dulan blood is one hundred percent orneriness, and you will find it when you need it. Besides, didn't you stand up to your grandfather and not marry that old man?" Willow asked.

"I guess I did." Velvet cocked her head to one side and grinned.

"See there," Willow said. "When you need it, it's there. It's just that you have the ability to curb your tongue better than I do so you don't need it so much."

Velvet chuckled.

"And what did you find out about me?" Garnet asked.

"That if I'm ever in a catfight or if a bunch of Indians ever raid this wagon train, I'd want you at my back. I believe you'd fight a forest fire with a china tea cup of water, with full intentions of putting it out," Willow said.

"She could just look at it and it would fade away beside all that red hair," Gussie laughed. "The man who gets her at the end of this trip better not be one of those dyed-in-the-wool fellers who think a woman hasn't got a brain and can't think for herself."

"That's the gospel according to Gussie," Garnet laughed.

"Want to know what I've found out?" Gypsy asked.

"Sure," Willow said.

"That Rafe Pierce is falling in love with you. His eyes search for you when you're not around and when you are, he pretends not to notice but he does," Gypsy whispered.

"You've got cow chips for brains," Willow laughed. "That man isn't capable of ever loving another woman."

"Oh, I know what you told us about that singer," Gypsy whispered very quietly, so Connie wouldn't hear. All they needed was for Connie to find out he wasn't married after all and poor old Rafe wouldn't be able to run far enough or long enough to get away from her. "He might not even know it yet, but it's the truth."

"Sure it is," Willow said. "Nature is calling. I'm going to drop back a little bit. If Rafe has ridden forward to talk to Hank, keep him busy until I catch up. Won't be but a minute."

"Changing the subject?" Gussie asked.

"Of course not," Willow said. "The subject doesn't even bear thinking about, let alone changing. If you let Rafe catch me with my skirt up, I'll never forgive you, so you better keep an eye out for him."

Willow found a bush and lifted her skirts. She remembered complaining to Aunt Harriet about having to run down the path to the outhouse, especially in the winter time. What she'd give right then for a little house couldn't be measured in promises or prayers. She'd already started back toward the last wagon when she heard a strange sound, carried to her ears on the south wind. She cocked her head to one side and listened so intently that her ears hurt. Nothing.

"Must have been a bird," she mumbled as she pulled the hem of her blue and white gingham checked skirt from a briar. Carefully, she stepped away from the tangled, spiny vine before it tore the hem right out of her skirt. The sound came again . . . a pitiful wailing so far away she could barely make it out. It had to be a bird, an odd one that they didn't have in Pennsylvania. Maybe one of those big white things that meandered around with the cattle.

What if it's a hurt person? she asked herself as she watched the train moving right along, away from her. *Rafe will deliver my head to Hank on a silver tray if I get lost.* She sighed.

"It won't take long. I'll keep the wagons in sight," she promised herself as she started a fast trot to the south. Every few feet, she'd stop long enough to make sure the noise was still there, and it always was, each time just a little louder than the time before.

She checked over her shoulder; the train was getting farther and farther away. Suddenly, it occurred to her that this could be a trap. Renegade Indians waiting to ambush the train and sending some kind of howls to their counterparts to relay messages. She turned around and started back to the train, which was at least a half a mile away by then. She argued with herself that if she didn't run she'd be until supper time catching up to the wagons. But the sound was closer this time, and she couldn't let some poor soul lie out there and die if she could help.

The wagons looked like toys by the time she heard the sound again. This time it really *was* close, and she could tell it wasn't a bird. It was the haunting sad weeping of someone whose heart was broken. Then it stopped and there was nothing but snuffles of fear.

"Where are you?" Willow asked gently. "Who are you? I'll help if I can."

Still there was nothing but the closed-mouth sobs of someone trying not to cry. Willow sat down on a log and listened carefully, scanning the area just as cautiously. "I'm here to help," she said. "I'm from a wagon train with lots of people. Can you come out from wherever you are and let me help you?"

A movement right under her posterior caused Willow to jump up at the same time a small child crawled out from inside the hollow log. "I'm scared," the little girl said, big brown eyes brimming with tears and dirt smudging every inch of her skin.

Willow opened her arms and the child stepped into them, weeping so loudly that it broke Willow's heart in half. Tears streamed down the dirty little cheeks and she wiped at them with a grimy hand. Her stomach rumbled and she began to gag.

"Here now." Willow patted her head. "You're going to be fine. Can you walk with me to the wagon train?"

"I can't go to the wagon train. They killed them all. They're all dead. Aunt Sue and Uncle Jasper. They shot them and they're dead. They took all the oxes and the stuff out of the wagons and went away. I was out picking flowers and I saw them do it, and I ran and ran and ran. We can't go to the wagon train. It's burned down. Are you an angel?"

"No, darling, I'm not an angel. We've got another wagon train, though, and you and I are going to go to it." Willow picked the child up, cuddled her against her breast and started walking. She'd do well to get back before they made camp. She just hoped her sisters didn't get worried and tell Rafe to come looking for her.

"Think of the devil, and he shall appear," she muttered to herself when she looked up and saw the big black horse riding her way.

"The devils are the ones who killed them all." The child clung to her even tighter.

"Indian devils?" Willow asked.

"No, they were just devils. But they laughed when they shot my aunt and uncle," the little girl said.

"What do you mean, lagging back this far?" Rafe began to shout before he got to her. "Are you stupid, Willow Dulan?"

"No, and you can quit your yelling," she said.

The child looked up at Rafe, buried her head in Willow's shoulder, and set up an ear-splitting howl. "That's the kind of devils they were. They rode black horses and yelled and yelled at Aunt Sue to tell them where she and Uncle Jasper hid their money in the wagon. I was going to go get it for them so they'd go away, but then they just shot them and I ran away."

"Where did you get that, and what's going on, Willow?" Rafe asked incredulously.

"You heard her. Their train was robbed and all the people killed. She got away and I heard her whimpering so I went to find her," Willow said. "Take her back to the camp and I'll catch up. Tell Velvet to take care of her."

"I don't think so," Rafe said.

"You are crazy as a one-eyed mule if you think I'm going to leave this baby in this wilderness, Rafe Pierce."

"I didn't say that," Rafe said. "It's only a mile or so. Buster can carry that much weight if we don't run him. Here, give me the girl and she can ride in front of me. You can ride behind."

"No! Don't give me to the devil man. He'll shoot me," the child cried.

"He's not a devil. Matter of fact, he was named for an angel. His name is Rafe and he'll be very careful with you. And when we get to the wagons, I bet Velvet will even have a biscuit for you." Willow soothed the child, rubbing her filthy little face with the tips of her fingers.

"But you'll be right there behind me?" she asked.

"Yes, right behind this big old angel. I promise I won't leave you." Willow handed her up to Rafe and then took his hand, letting him hoist her up in the saddle behind him. She wrapped her hands around his chest and laid them gently on the child's shoulders to reassure her that she was indeed right behind her.

Willow liked the feel of Rafe's strong back pressed against her chest. Someday, when he got over his heartbreak, some woman would ride with him like this, and he'd be a happy man again. A jealous streak shot through Willow's heart and she gave herself a thorough lecture. Her sisters weren't going to implant such a crazy idea in her mind. She had nothing to be jealous of because there was nothing there. Gypsy, with all the love stars in her eyes, wasn't going to convince her otherwise. No, she wouldn't listen to their silly talk. Not now. Not ever.

Rafe could have ridden all day with Willow's arms tightly around him. Somehow since they'd shared that kiss and their stories that night, the chains surrounding his heart had loosened. He was ready, at twenty-five, to think again about a woman in his life. For that, he probably owed Willow another thank-you, but that was one she'd never get. Rafe was willing to admit he could possibly fall in love and take a woman to his ranch, but it sure wouldn't ever be anyone like Willow Dulan. No siree, when he got serious and went looking for a wife this time, it would be a plain country girl with dark hair. Maybe with blue eyes like Willow's, or similar anyway. Only a Dulan would have those peculiar aqua-colored eyes.

"What happened?" Garnet propped her hands on her hips when Rafe reached the last wagon in the train. "What you got there besides our sister?"

"Got a child," Rafe said tersely. "If you'll get down, I'll hand her to you and go find Hank. I expect we can leave her at the Hollenberg Stage Station. We'll be there by supper tomorrow."

"No, don't leave me!" The child began to cry again when Rafe handed her to Willow.

"Now, look what you did," Willow accused, her blue eyes wide with pent-up anger. "You're not leaving this child anywhere."

"Promise!" The little girl hiccuped. "You said he was an angel and he wouldn't be mean."

"What in the devil is going on?" Garnet asked.

"Annie!" The child broke loose from Willow's grasp and ran into Annie's arms.

"Well, Merry Allie Briley, what on earth are you doing here? And why are you so dirty?"

"And I'm hungry too, Annie. I ain't had a bite to eat in two days," Merry clung to Annie. "Don't let that angel man leave me at a station. Please, Annie, don't let them take me away again."

"Of course I won't." Annie glared at Rafe. "You can stay right here with me and these sweet women and we'll take you to California with us. And that's a promise."

"Don't be making promises you can't keep," Rafe growled. "Hank will make the decision about what to do with this kid."

Annie drew herself up to her full five feet ten inches and picked Merry up, cradling her against her shoulder. "You and Hank can both jump off the nearest cliff. This child is staying with me, and if Hank don't like it then Hank can leave us both at Hollenberg Stage Station. I won't leave her."

"We'll see." Rafe rode off in a huff. Lord Almighty, that's all they needed. A little girl in the midst of all the women. Hank wouldn't have it, he was sure. Or was he? He'd been sure Hank wouldn't sign on those Dulan women either. Well, this issue was ironclad. No children. That had been Hank's decision from the beginning. Widows were fine but there'd be no children on the train. If they had kids, then he turned them away.

Annie began to walk as if she were carrying no more than a feather fan to keep the flies and gnats away from her face. She wouldn't leave this child to the mercy of strangers. "Connie," she said after a few minutes, when she heard Merry's stomach grumble, "go in the wagon and get me a biscuit. A plain one with no meat in it. She'll have to eat slowly here at first or it'll come back up."

"Yes, ma'am." Connie obeyed for the first time without a two-hour complaint. She picked up the extra tin cup she'd bought just in case Rafe ever came to dinner and filled it half full of water from one of the jars and took it with her. She hopped off the back of the moving wagon without spilling a drop.

"Okay, now Merry, I want you to sip this water. Slowly, now, child, and eat this biscuit. Little bites and chew them twenty times each so you won't get sick. Easy, now, keep walking with me while you eat." Annie set her down and Merry did just what she'd been told.

"How do you know her?" Willow asked. One portion of her heart was overrun with envy that Merry had abandoned her so quickly. After all, she was the one who'd saved her. The other portion was relieved that Merry had found a familiar face among them.

"Got to know her in the Patee House. Her aunt and uncle were heading up a little train with only five wagons. They weren't going far. Just south of Alcove Springs to some farmland they'd bought. Her aunt told me Merry was her niece's child. She had no other living relatives and they'd taken her in to raise. I won't let strangers have her, Willow. Not even if I have to give up my place and stay with her. She's mine now. You got a problem with that?"

"No ma'am, I surely do not. I'm just glad she knew somebody here and that you feel like that about her," Willow said.

The whole train knew the story by the time supper was finished. Annie gave Merry a bath in a small creek that ran along beside the campsite and Willow was amazed to see the child had light brown hair and a sprinkling of freckles across her nose. Willow volunteered to wash her soiled and torn dress while Annie brushed her hair. Merry was a midget inside Annie's shirt, but it didn't matter. There was sparkle back in the child's eyes and Willow would be willing to bet that in two days, the dark circles would be gone.

"Hank says no children," Rafe said from the creek bank, startling Willow so badly she almost tumbled into the water herself.

"Then Hank better get ready to lose Annie and she's a good woman. Sensible. Kind-hearted and keeps that mouthy Connie in line," Willow said.

"Guess that's his decision." Rafe shrugged. "We sent

Bobby back to see what could be done about the wagons. He'll be back in the morning. Might be there's survivors and she can go on with her kin."

"I don't think so," Willow said coldly. "Don't you like kids?"

"Sure, I love 'em. Even helped Hank on some trains with them, but not this one. This is a special one. Menfolks at the other end are waiting for brides, Willow. They ain't wanting to raise somebody else's kids."

"Any of those men got kids?" she asked.

"Sure, the preacher has three or four, I think. And a couple of others, maybe more that a couple had wives who died so they've got some kids they're needing help with," Rafe said.

"What's the difference? What's good for the goose should be good for the gander. Tell you what." She started poking him in the chest with each word like she'd done the first time they'd argued. "You tell Hank if that little girl stays, then the Dulan sisters stay, too."

"Well, hallelujah!" Rafe snapped. "If I'd known all we had to do was find an orphan to get rid of you, I mighta been tempted to burn a few wagons myself."

The palm of Willow's hand answered his insolence. She hoped his face burned all night as she stomped back to the circle of wagons. Drat his black soul to the backside of hell for that hateful, mean remark. Little Merry might be right. He just could be the devil instead of an angel.

Chapter Ten

Willow slept fitfully through the night and when the first rays of sun bounced off the scrub ash in the distance she was already up and dressed, waiting for the hustle in the men's camp outside the circle to begin. When she saw Hank's tall, lanky silhouette stoking up a fire, she stepped across the wagon tongue and started in that direction. No sooner had she reached the supply wagon that headed up the wagon train every day than Bobby came riding into the camp.

"Hank?" she and Bobby both spoke at the same time. Hank looked from one to the other. The prickly itch began on his neck. One or both of them was about to tell him something he for sure didn't want to know.

"What are you doing here?" Rafe asked Willow gruffly, tossing the last dregs of the coffee from the night before onto the ground and starting a new pot.

"I'm not here to talk to you," Willow said bluntly. "Hank, I've come to discuss something with you."

Hank looked from her to Bobby, who waited patiently. "Just a minute, Willow." Hank held up his hand. "What'd you find?" he asked Bobby.

"Just what the little girl told Annie and Willow, here. Burned wagons. People dead. It wasn't Indians. Had the mark of dirty white boys all over it. Signs said that they took the livestock back to St. Joe, where they'll probably sell them for a high dollar. The wagons would've been too much trouble and would slow them down. So they were burned. Nothing but bodies and ashes. I spent the night burying the dead. That little girl would've been dead with them if she hadn't run away," Bobby said softly. "Reckon I could catch a nap in the supply wagon this morning?"

"Sure you can," Hank said. "Grab some grub and curl up. Henry, you'll scout today. Now what was it you wanted?" Hank turned toward Willow and the itch on his neck intensified by a hundred percent.

"It's about that little girl, Merry Briley. Annie says that if you make the child stay at Hollenberg Stage Station then she's staying with her. Rafe was of the opinion you wouldn't let a child go on with the train since that was your rules," she said.

"Well, that's the rules." Hank rubbed his neck.

"Then I'm here to tell you they're going to change. I don't know what your final decision has been up to this point. I don't want to know. But if you decide to leave them at the station, then I'm going to incite a riot amongst the women. We're going to stop the wagons and refuse to budge until that child and Annie can go with us," Willow said.

"That's blackmail!" Rafe's brown eyes drew down into mere slits, his eyebrows a heavy dark ledge above them. "Those women won't listen to you anyway. Maybe your hot-headed sisters, but not the whole bunch of them. Connie won't."

"Then Connie can drive all twenty-one wagons to California with you, and the bunch of you can explain to those waiting men how they would have had wives but you didn't want to burden any of them with an orphan child," she said stiffly. Mercy, Rafe's mother had sure enough made a mistake when she named him for a healing angel. She should have named him Damian or at least Luther; anything but Rafael, after an angel.

"I'll leave you with it, Hank. It's your decision. Not one of those women know I'm here to talk to you about this, so I'm not trying to usurp your authority. I'm just stating facts as I see them. Seems like if there's men there with children that these women are expected to raise for them, then there should be one man who's not adverse to raising an orphan," Willow said. "We'll be ready to roll in half an hour. I noticed the girls are already frying up last night's beans into patties for the nooning. If you got anything to say to us before we go, then it might be a good time to say it pretty soon. If you don't, then I'll just figure that you decided to leave that child behind, and I'll speak my mind to the women. That's all I got to say."

"That's enough," Rafe said between clenched teeth.

"Yes, it is," Willow said. "It's your call, Hank."

"I told you." Rafe pointed a finger at Hank when Willow was barely out of earshot. "I told you those five would bring nothing but trouble."

"Yes, and I should've listened to you," Hank said, slapping his hat against his denim overalls. "But I didn't. And she's got a good point, you know. How could we live with ourselves if we just left that child at a stage station with no hopes of ever having a relative come rescue her?"

"Rules is rules," Rafe said. He didn't want to leave the child either, but he sure didn't want to admit Willow was right.

"Indians wouldn't even be having this conversation." Bobby yawned. "If they'd found that little girl, they'd have taken her home and made her one of their own."

Rafe glared at him and Hank chuckled. So rules were rules. He wouldn't break them but he might bend them slightly, and make even more. It was clearer than water in a bubbling brook that Rafe Pierce was having trouble with his own feelings about that youngest Dulan girl. He'd have to face his own demons in that area, Hank thought. No one else could take care of that business for him. Sure as shootin', that Willow was a handful and always would be, but something about her was right fetching. It must be that part that plumb had old Rafe's heart tied up in a double-hitched knot.

"I guess I'd better go have my talk. Rafe, I want you to come along with me," Hank said.

"No thanks." Rafe picked up his saddle and slung it over the blanket already on Buster's back.

"Please," Hank said. "Not that it's an order but I think it would do you good to hear what I'm going to tell those women."

"Oh, all right." Rafe dropped the saddle. "Let's go let Willow have her way."

"She might not want it once she gets it." Hank chuckled again. "Sometimes a body needs to be very, very careful what they pray for, 'cause when they get it, it sure ain't what they thought it would be."

"Which gospel did that come out of?" Rafe fought with a twitching at the corners of his mouth and lost the battle, his face breaking out in a wide grin.

"The one according to old Hank the wagon master." Hank led the way across dew-kissed grass to the circle of wagons, where the smell of bean cakes sizzling in the grease left from the morning bacon permeated through the crisp morning air. The bean cakes had been Velvet's idea the second or third morning on the trail when she'd seen the women tossing out the leftovers from the night before. She'd taught them to add equal amounts of flour and corn-meal to the leftover beans, pat them into cakes and fry them in the hot grease from the morning's breakfast. Most mornings the girls brought a bag full to him and the hired help, and Hank had sure grown to love those little patties when they stopped for a thirty-minute nooning to let the oxen graze a bit and rest.

Hank stepped up on a rain barrel that Gypsy had taken from the side of their wagon the night before to tip up for the last dregs of good water for a pitcher of tea. His tall, lanky frame reminded Willow of the stick figures children drew when they first started school. She noticed that he kept rubbing his neck and wondered briefly if he might have slept crooked the night before. Once he adjusted his spectacles and cleared his throat, he began to look like a real politician up there on his makeshift soapbox. Would he be a politician and try to wriggle his way out of this, or would he state his business and leave them to it? That's what Willow had decided to do: state her business and let each woman there make up their own mind as to which side they'd take up with.

"Ladies, could I have your attention for a moment?" he said, raising his voice over the buzz of the morning.

Willow stepped down from the back of the wagon and caught Rafe's eye. He didn't look a bit happy, but it didn't seem that he wanted to drop her dead with one look, either. If Rafe had talked Hank into abiding by his ironclad rules, then he would have had a much more smug look on his face. But then, if he been totally defeated, Willow was sure he wouldn't even be standing there. She was at a complete loss where the men were concerned. Was Hank going to tell them that Annie and Merry had to stay at the station after all?

"We have a bit of a problem," Hank said when everyone was quiet and listening. "The child Willow rescued has created this problem. The rules in the contract you each signed says no children. It's not that any of us hate kids or that the men on the other end of this line hate them either. Some of those fellows have children that you will be responsible to help finish raising. I made that rule and I won't break it. Kids slow trains down. They're more apt to be sick than adults. They whine and they demand attention. Like I said, I won't break it, but I will bend it. Because Merry Briley has no relatives to come and claim her, according to the conversations her aunt had with Annie, I'm going to let her travel with us. But these are the new rules.

Annie, you are responsible for this child if she's going to be your adopted daughter. If she goes off picking wildflowers and we lose an hour hunting her—and it can happen easily, I know, I've brought lots of trains across this land—then the next day the whole bunch of you will walk an extra five miles. We are up to twelve miles a day now and stopping just at sunset. Add five miles to that and we'll be stopping at bedtime or later. So we'll keep the child. The Indians say that it takes a village to raise a child. I'm telling you, it'd better take a hundred and seven women to keep this one child in line. Put her on a wagon seat with a different wagon every day or let her walk, but we won't lose a mile because of Miss Merry Briley. Is that understood?"

Rafe grinned and Willow's hand tingled with the desire to slap thunder out of his handsome face. She'd put up with a stinging, even bruised hand, just for a moment of instant gratification. Well, he could just take his insolent smile and ride a hot poker to the front gates of hell with it. Willow Dulan would carry that child all the way to California just to prove him wrong.

"Understood." Annie smiled brightly at Hank. "And thank you, Hank."

"Thank you, Mr. Hank," Merry said brightly. "I'll be good. I promise."

"I'm sure you will." Hank reached out and tousled the child's curly hair. "But if you aren't, and we have to walk extra miles to make up the time, you just remember that you caused it."

"She'll be good," Annie said, taking the child by the hand and leading her back to the wagon. "Now let's get that hair braided and today you can ride on the seat with me. It'll be a long day but we'll tell each other stories."

Rafe brushed past Willow, his arm touching her bare one and sending exploding sparks all around her. She assured herself that they were not tingles of desire for that abominable man, but rather the byproducts of glowing rage. He told himself that the slow burn in the depths of his heart wasn't anything near infatuation; it was merely the after effects of a battle that neither side had really won. Willow Dulan might win a battle or two on the way to Ash Hollow, where he'd bid them all an ecstatic good-bye, but she sure wouldn't win the war.

Rafe wandered into the narrow five-room building where Hollenberg sold supplies, meals, and lodging to travelers coming from the St. Joseph branch of the Oregon-California Trail. He was a native of Germany and had actually spent several years searching for gold, but in the end, he'd found more money could be made selling supplies to people on their way to the promised land. Little did they realize there wasn't a promised land. Just a pretty state with some gold hidden down deep, but finding those elusive gold nuggets was as difficult as pulling hen's teeth. Mr. Hollenberg and his wife worked hard at their trade, but it wasn't anything compared to panning or digging for gold.

Rafe had actually gone inside with intentions of buying Merry a cup of her own, but no sooner had it in his hand, than he overheard Annie telling her that she didn't need a cup since they'd bought an extra one at the Indian Mission. He put the cup back on the shelf and was looking at bright colored ribbons when he backed right into Willow, who was fingering a bolt of calico.

"Excuse me," he said before he even looked over his shoulder to see who he'd bumped into.

"What are you doing in here?" she asked. She couldn't step backwards. Her hips were already pressed firmly into the table holding the bolts of fabric. If she stepped forward she would literally be in his arms. A slow blush began on the back of her neck and wiggled its way upward, putting high color into her cheeks.

Rafe could have taken one step back and given her some space, but she was so beautiful standing there in her faded calico day dress, a rebellious blond curl or two trying to escape the confines of the bun on the nape of her neck. Time stood still as he stared into her mesmerizing blue eyes and wished he could touch the soft flesh on her red cheeks. "I'm buying supplies," he said in a hoarse whisper. "Any law against that?"

Willow couldn't answer. For the first time she was totally speechless. His deep, low voice hypnotized her. There were no other people in the whole store, in the whole world. Just Rafe Pierce. With his dark hair and those haunting brown eyes that drew her into his very soul. Somehow he'd reached out and touched her elbow and she braced herself for the kiss that was on its way.

"Oh, Rafe." Connie's voice broke the magic spell. "I'm going to purchase some walking boots. Mine have a hole in the sole of each foot. Would you please come with me over here and tell me which is the better buy?"

"Just find a pair that fits well," he said gruffly, without taking his eyes off Willow.

"But I need you to help me." She grabbed him by the arm and dragged him across the room to the shelves where Mr. Hollenberg displayed the shoes. "Do I want these black ones or these brown ones? Or would a pair of man-looking boots like Willow wears be best?"

Rafe couldn't help but tilt his head down and look at Willow's feet. Sure enough, boots very similar to the ones he wore peeked out from the hem of her skirt. Men's clothing. Men's boots. Faded calico. Nothing to recommend her and yet he couldn't stop dreaming of her at night. Or seeking her out through the day just to see what she was doing. Yes, sir, it certainly was a good thing he was only going with this train to Ash Hollow. For the next two and a half weeks he'd have to watch his step a little closer. Then when he got home he would begin to seriously look for a wife. One who'd be content on his ranch. One he could trust with his heart and his future. One totally unlike Willow Dulan with all her sass and independence.

Willow took a deep breath and busied herself with the

calico. Hopefully, no one else saw that public tête-à-tête. Especially one of her sisters. After a few moments, she chanced a scanning of the store, and was relieved to find everyone busy with their own business and not looking at her like she was some kind of loose woman. What would she have done if he had leaned forward and kissed her right there in the store? She honestly couldn't answer that question, but she knew down deep she'd have to be very careful because she lost control when Rafe was that close. She'd just have to be on her toes every moment to see to it an incident like that didn't happen again.

Late that evening they stopped for the night along a shallow creek so the women could have baths and wash their clothing. Willow was among the first to get her laundry done and the first to take her bath. A smug little feeling settled down in her chest as she watched the sunset in the west, thinking of all those miners in the town of Bryte waiting impatiently for their wedded bliss to begin. They'd be watching the same sunset. Would there be one who liked to stop at the end of a long day's work and sit quietly in awe on the back porch as the day faded into night? Or would she be matched up with a coarse man who thought sunsets were just tomfoolery? A sad, lost feeling replaced the smugness of the idea that she'd thwarted any accidents with Rafe Pierce. How would she ever live with a man who didn't appreciate God's beautiful palette? She shook off the attitude with the thought that she'd simply see to it that there were enough women for the men. That way she and her sisters could go on to another town and find jobs of some kind. Maybe they'd start their own hotel or restaurant. All of them had a fine hand in the culinary arts. Then someday a man would arrive in her world who loved her *and* pretty sunsets.

"Whatever cloud are you riding on?" Garnet broke into her thoughts.

"Oh, one where everything is beautiful," Willow said.

"Well, stop the world and let me crawl up there with

you." Garnet laughed. "I do believe little Merry is going to be the best-dressed woman on the train. We should have all had a conference before we bought material for dresses today. Annie bought her a new pair of walking shoes, and she ended up with stuff to make six dresses. Velvet is out there right now cutting down a pattern and laying it on the fabric. Merry is dancing around like a gypsy when the music starts."

"Do you suppose that the reason five of those pieces of calico got bought is that there's five sisters who remember what it's like to be shifted from pillar to lamp post, as Gussie said?" Willow asked.

"Probably." Gussie hopped out of the back of the wagon. "Merry is good for all of us. She makes us forget about the struggles of the trip. She's riding with me on the wagon seat tomorrow. I'm really looking forward to it. By the time we all get to Bryte, I bet we're itching for daughters of our own."

"The Lord works in mysterious ways," Gypsy said quietly. "Maybe He gave Merry to us to help us, rather than us helping her."

"Probably. Make her wear those shoes all day tomorrow, Gussie. Even though she's on the wagon seat, make her wear them so they'll begin to mold to her foot. That way when she walks in them she won't get blisters," Willow said. Then she remembered her own boots . . . she'd left them beside the creek. She'd meant to pick them up with the wet clothing she'd washed after her bath, but in her rush to get back to camp—to avoid a run-in with Rafe— she'd forgotten them.

"I'll do it," Gussie said. "Thought I might ask Velvet for all the scraps of that piece of material and let her cut them out into diamonds for a lone star quilt top. She's not too young to learn a fine stitch. It'll give her something to work on while she's with me, and if she gets tired of the hard wagon seat, she can sit on the pillows in the back and work on her quilt."

They were still talking about whether Merry should start a lone star quilt, or if a log cabin might be simpler for a beginner, when Willow picked her heavy heart up and started back down to the creek to retrieve her boots. She checked the men's camp but couldn't tell which of the dark silhouettes belonged to which man. No doubt Hank was the skinny one with the glow of the fire reflecting off his eyeglasses. But the rest of the men were either sitting hunched up, drinking coffee and talking quietly, or stretched out on the ground, using their saddles for pillows.

"That would be Rafe," she mumbled. "Asleep. Like I would be, if I hadn't forgotten my boots."

She tiptoed barefoot through the grass to the place she'd claimed for her bath and washing. The sun barely had a half circle left on the horizon and she was watching the brilliant oranges fade outward into peach and apricot rays against the clouds scuttling across the deep blue sky when she stepped on a broken twig. She grabbed her bare foot in one hand and hopped around, stifling a scream that would bring the whole camp running to her rescue. That's all she needed. Rafe and Bobby, along with Hank, to thrash through the brush with their guns drawn. Not to mention a bruise on the bottom of her foot to ache all the next day. Of all the days, when she would be walking, not driving.

"Looking for these?" Rafe held up a pair of boots right in front of her nose during her silent stomp dance.

"Just give them to me." She gritted her teeth. "I had my hands full and forgot to pick them up."

He carefully put them in her hands, trying very hard not to let his fingertips touch hers. But she didn't get a grip on one of them and it fell between them. They both bent to pick it up at the same time and in the darkness his hand closed on hers. He looked up from a bowed position to find her face scarcely inches from his. The next few seconds passed in slow motion for both of them. It took a hundred years for them to stand upright again; another hundred for him to tilt her chin back and kiss her, drinking in the sweetness of freshly washed skin and desire. The kiss itself lasted only a moment and then both of them pulled back in embarrassment. They'd vowed to themselves that this wouldn't happen again.

Willow hurriedly picked up her boot and held it close to her shawl. "Thank you for finding them," she said stiffly. Emotions exploded inside her heart like shooting stars. She would never let Rafe know how much his kisses affected her. She couldn't even admit that to herself.

"I came out here where it was peaceful to watch the setting of the sun. I love that time of day. Work hard and clean up, then sit down and watch the day go away into dusk. Seems only fitting to give a little time to see the glorious displays and not take them for granted, when God has been so gracious as to give them to us. Found your boots and figured I'd just set them beside your wagon," Rafe said, his voice much deeper than usual.

"I agree about the sunset. Good night, Rafe. And thank you again for finding my boots." Willow walked away from him. She touched her lips, trying to hold the kiss there forever, along with the wonderful feeling deep in her heart that went with it.

Walking away from Rafe was much more difficult than the day she had left Pete Hanson standing on the wooden sidewalk outside the stage station in Mercersburg, Pennsylvania. Part of her wanted to turn around and rush back into his arms. To beg him to kiss her one more time. A planned kiss to see if every time their lips met the whole world went up in a blaze of fire. The other part knew she had to run away as fast as she could from the feelings she was experiencing. Nothing could ever come of it. Not with Rafe Pierce. He wanted some kind of sweet little wife to walk three steps behind him all day long and never speak her mind. He surely didn't want someone like Willow Dulan. Everything in his eyes said he despised everything about her most of the time. Only when she was in his arms with his lips on hers did they get along. It was nothing more than a silly schoolgirl infatuation, and she'd have to wake up from her trail-weary boredom and face the facts.

Suddenly, she wondered—did Pete ever watch a sunset? She knew the answer in her own soul by the time she got back to the camp. Pete Hanson would never watch sunsets with anyone but Lucy. He might marry a respectable woman someday, but it wouldn't be for love. Willow might marry someday, but only if it was for love. So there had better be a hundred healthy women alive and willing to marry up with a man they'd never met when they arrived in Bryte. Because even if Willow had to disappear in the dark, probably with Garnet, she wasn't marrying any man she didn't love.

"Miss Willow, come and see what Velvet done cut out for me." Merry grabbed her hand as soon as she stepped inside the circle of wagons. "It's got a little yellow flower in the material and guess what, Miss Willow? Uncle Rafe bought me a yellow ribbon for my hair just to match it. He said all my curls needed a yellow ribbon. Isn't it beautiful?"

"Yes, it is." Willow smiled at the child's exuberance. "Did I hear you call him Uncle Rafe?"

"Yes you did. Uncle Rafe and Uncle Hank. They said I could call them Uncle since I don't have any uncles any more. I can't wait until my dress is all made. Annie says I might have to save it for Sunday but Uncle Rafe says I should wear it and be pretty for everyone. And Uncle Hank says there ain't Sundays west of St. Joe, Missouri, so I might get to wear it when she gets finished sewing it." Merry chattered on until Annie called her to say her prayers and go to bed.

"Uncle Rafe!" Willow exclaimed.

"Kinda cute, ain't it?" Gypsy said. "Sounds a lot better than Angel Rafe, don't it?"

"Hmmph," Willow all but snorted. "I'm going to make out my bed and go to sleep."

She made out the bed and settled her head on the pillow.

Carolyn Brown

Sleep didn't arrive until the moon was high in the sky though, as she replayed the emotional upheaval in her breast when Rafe kissed her. Would she ever find another man who made her feel like that?

Chapter Eleven

"Miss Willow, Miss Willow, come and see." Merry hopped around like a grasshopper and pointed toward the rising sun. Six wagons were silhouetted against the sky not far from their own circle, and Merry was pointing with one finger, yellow braids flopping with every jump. "Do you think they've got any kids? Wonder if they'll come up here and talk to us? Do you reckon they'll join up with our train? What do you think they'll be like?"

"Mercy, Merry!" Willow laughed. "I wouldn't know a thing about them."

"Yes, they have kids." Rafe stepped over the wagon tongue and opened his arms. Merry made a running jump and wrapped herself around him. "And yes, Merry, they're going to come over here and talk to us, but they aren't going to join the train except for a day, then they'll split off on their own journey to Utah. But tonight Hank has agreed that we can stop an hour early and have a bit of fun. There's a fiddle player with them and we can dance and visit. So does that answer your questions?"

"Yes, Uncle Rafe. Can I go tell everyone else?" Merry looked at him as if he were really an angel dropped out of heaven.

Willow glared at both of them. The women took care of

117

Merry and loved her dearly. And she gave back love in abundance, but not a one of them could make Merry's eyes twinkle like her Uncle Hank or Uncle Rafe. Neither of whom ever braided that unruly hair or sewed calico dresses for her. All they did was tell her stories and make her giggle. It just plain wasn't fair.

"Are they going to head up the train or travel behind it?" Merry cocked her head to one side and made plans in her own little mind.

"Travel behind it, so I'd suggest you wrangle an invitation to ride in with Miss Willow today so you can play with any children who might want to run ahead and get acquainted with you. But you better remember what Hank said last week when you joined up with this train. Get lost or cause us to have to stop and there'll be a punishment for sure." Rafe kissed her on the forehead and set her down.

Willow coveted that kiss for a few seconds then gave herself a severe scolding for thinking such thoughts. Her eyebrows knit into a solid line across her forehead, where wrinkles furrowed in fine lines. Her mouth drew up into a tight little bow as she watched Merry run from one wagon to the other delivering the news.

"So you don't relish the idea of company?" Rafe asked gruffly.

"I love the idea of company and of a party tonight," Willow said, jerking her head up to stare right into his eyes. Mistake. Big mistake. Every time she did that she lost control, and losing control scared Willow Gail Dulan even more than spiders and snakes.

"Could've fooled me," Rafe growled. "Look on your face said you hated the idea."

"All goes to prove that a man can't read a woman's expressions as well as he thinks he can. Good day, Mr. Pierce," Willow said. She picked up her bedding and began to make a neat roll.

Rafe stormed off toward the men's camp. Lord, but he'd like to strangle that woman. He put his hands out in front of him and locked his fingers in a fierce grip as he pretended to throttle the life out of Willow Dulan. But somewhere in the middle of the dastardly deed her eyes appeared before him, and he dropped his hands to his sides. She melted all the cold chains around his heart one moment and the very next turned into a statue of ice herself. She was the only woman who'd awakened his emotions since that day he'd walked into his own house and found out what a fool he'd been. Thinking that Rachel Throckmorton could actually love a dirt farmer and rancher like him.

"Make you mad again, did she? I think you may have to take her home with you or live in misery the rest of your life," Bobby taunted when Rafe got back to camp.

"You better hope your Indian blood tells the truth when it comes to scouting us out good trails, because it's lying to you if it's telling you that," Rafe said, picking up his saddle blanket and throwing it over his big black horse. "If I took that woman home with me, I'd be guaranteed a life of pure misery. All we do is fight."

Willow stomped the ground so hard that dust boiled up around her skirt. It's a good thing she didn't carry her gun in a holster on her hip. The temptation would be too blasted great to just put a hole right between Rafe Pierce's gorgeous eyes. She'd show him and get over him at the same time. Tonight when they had a dance, she'd dance with any one of the men on that train who asked her. She'd barely washed all the disappointment from her heart concerning Pete when she and her sisters joined the wagon train and there was Rafe. Someone to stir up the emotions she thought she'd buried along with her heart when she found out she was little more than a brood mare to Pete. She wiped sweat from her brow but the tiny rivulet running between her breasts couldn't be touched. Not with the high-collared faded calico. Drat it all, she'd be a sweaty mess by the evening dance and there wouldn't be a fellow interested in dancing with her after all. She looked around at all the women in the camp, and then past them to the six lonesome little wagons. Probably six families with young children. Six men with six wives and a more than a hundred unmarried women. What ever made her think she'd stand a chance of even one dance? She shook her head and stomped her foot again.

"Got a little problem with Rafe again?" Velvet tucked things into the back of the wagon. "When you going to admit you are interested in that man?"

"Me, interested in that rogue?" Willow's voice was shrill with anger.

Velvet giggled. "The fact that he's a rogue is probably what piques your curiosity. The fact that you're a female rogue is what makes him keep coming back sniffing around this wagon."

"I'm not a female rogue," Willow protested. "I'm ... I'm ..."

"You are his match," Velvet finished the sentence for her. "Merry says we've got company and we get to have a visit and a party. Sounds wonderful, don't it?"

"It sure does." Willow gritted her teeth. It would be wonderful, too. It would be the most wonderful evening of her entire life because she was going to get over Rafe Pierce tonight. Dance or no dance. It was over. As of right now. Willow Gail Dulan wasn't going to have her heart broken again. No. Better to marry someone she didn't know and wasn't expected to ever really love than marry up with someone she cared deeply about and have her heart shredded into ribbons again. Forget that vow she'd made to herself a few days before—that she would never marry for anything but love. Men loved themselves. They loved their dogs. They loved their horses. And their kept women. How many of them really loved their wives?

Pete had been a genuine prophet and she hadn't realized it. It's just that he had been an honest prophet. For that she had to respect him. Once she knew about Lucy, he had stepped right up and admitted the situation. Most men probably kept a woman—their first love—in the shadows. Aunt

Harriet had been right all along. There wasn't a one of them worth more than the price of a bullet. The fact that it was against the law to shoot the sorry scoundrels was a pure pity.

"What's the matter with you?" Gussie asked as she took up the reins and slapped the oxen flanks. "You been fighting with Rafe again?"

"Yes, she has," Velvet answered. "What else can make her look like a thundercloud about to explode? And mercy me, but they can fight about the simplest things. Don't have to be anything big."

"I wonder if he kisses as passionately as he fights?" Gypsy fell into step with her two sisters. "What can you tell us, Willow?"

"I can't tell you nothing," Willow said, high color filling her cheeks until they burned bright red.

Garnet chuckled. "You don't lie so well, little sister. But don't worry about it. He'll be gone in a few days. Only until he gets us through Ash Hollow, you know. Then you've got the better part of seven months to get over the way he makes your little heart do double time."

Willow kept her eyes straight ahead and just nodded. She couldn't utter a word around the lump in her throat. Her heart missed a beat and fell down into the bottom of her boots. Every step she took ground it into an aching pulp. One step closer to Ash Hollow. She'd never see Rafe again. *Hallelujah*, her mind shouted. She wiped the tears from her eyes and hoped her sisters thought she was battling the dust from the other wagons. Her heart throbbed with pain. The was no peace for Willow Gail Dulan that day.

Merry and four little girls made a circle and danced to the fast tune the musician played. The fiddler had produced a banjo and a mandolin and asked if any of the wagon train crew or the ladies could play. Garnet stepped and up and took the banjo from his hands. She would have preferred a piano, but not many folks loaded a heavy piano onto their wagons when they started west. There'd been one fool who tried it for a while, but it hadn't lasted a week out of St. Joe. It had pained Garnet's heart the day they passed that piano sitting on the side of the trail. Rain and weather had rotted the wood and faded the ivory keys, but Garnet's fingers still itched just to stop long enough to see if she could coax a fast little barroom tune from what was left of that grand old piano.

Bobby said he'd try to keep up on the mandolin. Rafe raised an eyebrow, and Bobby informed him he'd learned to play a similar instrument when he was a child in his tribe. The music began and the women warmed up to each other and began to visit. Recipes were exchanged. Hardship stories told. Men discussed in whispers behind fans. Two long makeshift tables were laid out with pots of food: beans with ham, stewed potatoes, fried sweet potatoes, cornbread, hoecakes, several big apple cobblers with sugar sprinkled on the top, lots of black coffee, and even sweet tea.

Willow and Gypsy sat on the back of their wagon, watching the little girls and laughing at their antics. To be that young again, Willow thought, would be heavenly. No cares. No wrenching heart pain over a man who loved another woman so much he wouldn't even give her up for a wife; or one who was the devil reincarnated in spite of his angelic name.

"Excuse me, ma'am." A young man materialized in front of them, his big blue eyes on Willow. "My name is Malachi Brubaker and I'd sure be honored if you'd have this dance with me."

His chin was a bit weak. Not at all like Rafe's strong, slightly clefted chin. His eyes were a washed-out blue, with no deep dark secrets or hidden pain. He was at least five inches shorter than Rafe and built on a smaller frame that didn't have nearly the muscle tone. He wore his fine, light brown hair parted on the side, unlike Rafe, who finger-combed his thick dark hair straight back. Not one single thing to remind Willow of Rafe—and that's exactly what she wanted that evening.

"I'd be glad to dance with you Mr. Brubaker. My name is Willow Dulan and this is my sister, Gypsy Rose," she said, taking his proffered arm and letting him lead her out into the middle of the campsite.

She put one hand on his shoulder and placed the other in his bony, callused palm. He danced fairly well and there were no tingles crawling down her backbone as she followed his lead. Nothing to fill her cheeks with high color. Just a formal dance with a nice young man.

"So you one of the brides going to California?" He attempted conversation when the dance ended and he led her back to the wagon.

"Yes, I am," she answered.

"And your sister is going, too?"

"Yes, all five of us sisters," she said.

"Oh! Well, what did your family think of that?" he asked incredulously. Surely he'd misunderstood the number. The way he'd been raised, a family stayed together, from birth through eternity. They sure didn't let five girls go gallivanting out across the world in search of husbands.

"Not one thing," Gypsy laughed and answered for Willow. "We are the only family left. So we're traveling together and we're going to settle down in the same town together."

"I see," the young man said.

"Well, thank you again for the dance, Mr. Brubaker," Willow said, taking her arm from the crook of his and feeling the heat from Rafe's stare all the way across the camp. Surely she was misinterpreting what she felt. The heat from her own pent-up emotional upheaval was haunting her. That and dancing so near the campfire caused the flush around her cheeks and neck. It was not the result of Rafe's piercing glare.

"Just Baker, ma'am," he said. "Never did care much for Malachi but my father named all of us from the Bible.

Guess time he got to number fifteen he was running out of ideas. Anyway, most folks just call me Baker, and I'd be pleased if you'd do that, too."

"Fifteen!" Willow exclaimed.

"Yep," he said with a blush. He wasn't about to tell her that he wasn't the baby of the family either, or that the children didn't all share the same mother. No, he wouldn't tell her all the family secrets. Not just yet. Not when he planned to marry Willow Dulan. She'd make him a fine first wife. By next year, when they had a child, she'd understand the way things were meant to be, and then he'd marry Esther, the young girl he was already engaged to. Esther wouldn't mind waiting a year. She was only sixteen and that would give her one more year with her parents. Esther was a real beauty. Long, dark hair and big round brown eyes. She'd been the love of his life since the first time he laid eyes on her. But Esther was shy and would never do as a first wife, who needed to fill the place of authority. Miss Willow Dulan had that look about her. The one that said she could step up to the job and take care of it. And she was so beautiful, with those long blond curls and strange aqua-colored eyes. It would certainly be no hardship to slip between the sheets with her every night for a year while he waited to wed Esther.

"And where is all your family?" Willow asked.

"Oh, they've all gone on to Utah. I stayed behind to help bring this little train. Most of them are relatives. The fiddler is my uncle and the man over there with the long black beard is my cousin. Miss Willow, are you really going to marry some man you don't know?" he asked.

Willow glanced toward Rafe. His eyes bored holes through the space separating them. His arms were folded tightly across his chest and she could almost see the muscles in his jaws working in anger. *Well, what does he have to be mad about*? she asked herself. All she was doing was talking to this kid. She wasn't about to run off to Utah with him!

"Yes, I guess I will if there's enough men to go around. You see, we signed on as a kind of insurance policy. If there's a hundred women then we'll step down and not have a husband when we get there. If there is less than a hundred then we'll be counted among the brides," she said.

"I see," he said. "Well, thank you for the dance. I think I'll go and talk to Mr. Hank. We've got some business to take care of."

She watched the other young men from the wagons dance with the ladies. The evening was festive and a real luxury after weeks of traveling with no diversions.

"Fifteen," she whispered, shaking her head.

"Fifteen what?" Rafe said from right behind her, the warmth of his breath on her neck fairly well curling her toenails with desire. Anger boiled up from the tips of her shoes. Why did her body have to respond to his touch like that? It plain wasn't fair. The worst possible match for her in the whole world—even worse than Pete—and her silly body ached for just the feel of his gaze upon her face, for his mouth on hers, for the feel of his arms holding her tightly against his broad chest.

"Kids. That boy comes from fifteen kids," she said. "I can't imagine that many kids in one household. The poor mother."

Rafe smiled. Chances were there were more than fifteen, but chances were also good that there were four or five mothers. Didn't Willow know why those folks in those six wagons were headed to Utah, and why there were more women to each wagon than men folks?

"Care to dance?" He changed the subject.

"Are you asking?" She raised an eyebrow.

"Yes, ma'am, I most certainly am." Rafe crooked his arm.

"Go on." Gussie fanned herself with the back of her hand as an older man led her back to the wagon. "It's the most fun we've had since we left, honey. Don't waste a single minute of music time just standing around visiting. Even that apple cobbler can't compare to a good dance, so go dance, Willow." She pushed her sister toward Rafe, who caught her in his arms as she tumbled forward. Sparks twinkled around them so brightly the stars paled in comparison.

They moved to the music with such grace that the other people stopped and watched. Willow blushed at the attention but could have no more stopped dancing with Rafe, or looking up into his mesmerizing brown eyes, than she could have sprouted wings and flown straight up to heaven.

Baker watched them and stiffened his resolve to have Willow for a wife. He inched over to Hank and asked him if he had plenty of hired hands to get the wagon train to Independence Rock.

"Why you askin' son?" Hank eyed the young man.

"Well, I figured I could help out to that point then go on up to where I'm headed. Make a little money to add to what I got to start up my own homestead when I get there," Baker said.

"And besides, you got your eye on Willow Dulan, ain't you?" Hank said with a deep chuckle.

"Yes, sir, I surely have at that," Baker replied firmly.

Hank set his jaw for a few minutes. Maybe that's what it would take to make his friend Rafe open his eyes and see what all the other boys already knew. Besides, Hank could always use an extra hand when they got to Ash Hollow. Lord Almighty, that was going to be a trial getting all the wagons down that holler. He'd be lucky if he didn't lose a woman or two in that horrendous job.

"Reckon I could use you up to Independence Rock," Hank said. "But you better be advised that these women have all signed a contract to be wives to men in California. Miss Willow Dulan is not up for grabs, son."

"Yes, sir, but you got five more than you need. If she was to decide to go on with me past Independence Rock, would you stand in her way?" Baker asked.

"We'd have to think on that long and hard," Hank said. By that time Willow wouldn't even be around if Hank's scheme worked out. If that bullheaded Rafe didn't open his heart, then Hank would tell Willow himself that if she agreed to go with Baker she'd most likely be one of many wives.

"Fair enough." Baker grinned and went off to tell his uncle his new plans.

"You dance well," Rafe said, looking deeply into Willow's aqua eyes.

"Thank you, Rafe. You don't do so poorly yourself," she said as the music ended.

When the dance ended, Garnet declared she needed a break and something to drink. She dipped up a cup of tea from the wooden bucket on the table. It was lukewarm but it tasted like the angels had kissed it, with just a faint taste of real lemon and sugar. She joined Willow, both of them leaning back against the side slats of the oversized wagon.

"Ever see so many kids?" Willow asked.

"These people believe in lots of kids. They kind of took that business about 'go ye forth and multiply' seriously," Garnet said.

"I guess they did." Willow smiled.

"You and that Rafe Pierce surely do dance good together. Bet if you'd stop fighting you'd find other things you could do good together," Garnet whispered.

"Garnet Diana." Willow blushed again. In all her life she could count the times she'd blushed bright red on one hand and not even use all the fingers. At least until she'd met Rafe Pierce. Seemed like lately she ran around with a red face most of the time.

"Well, it's the truth. Everyone knows it but you and that blabbermouth Connie. Look at her over there batting her eyes at him and flirting like a girl fresh out of short skirts." Garnet nodded toward Rafe, who looked bored to distraction.

"Good enough for him," Willow declared.

"And that fellow you danced with first. He appeal to you?" Garnet asked.

" 'Bout as much as a spider," Willow laughed.

The sound of her voice carried to Rafe, who whipped around to look at her. One time, just once, he'd like to make Willow laugh like that. He shut his eyes and imagined her coming in from the chicken yard on his ranch with the tail of her apron pulled up around her waist and filled with fresh eggs for his breakfast. She had a smile on her face and the sound of her laughter when she looked up at him on the back porch sounded just like that. He opened his eyes and ears at the same time to see Connie and hear her fussing at him petulantly for not listening to a word she'd been saying.

"Well, he's got eyes for you and I heard him ask Hank for a job," Garnet said. "I think we'll be seeing lots more of that boy in the next few days."

"You can have him." Willow felt the red embers of heat passing between her and Rafe. "I don't want him."

"Honey, I wouldn't either if I had a choice between him and Rafe Pierce. I'm not even so sure I'd hang onto my vow to not marry if one of those fellers out at the end of the rainbow looked a little like him." Garnet laughed.

"Well, jump right out there and flirt with Rafe, then," Willow snapped.

"I don't think so." Garnet shook her head. "Be a lost cause from the beginning."

Well, it is here, too, Willow thought as she watched her older sister pick up the banjo again and pick out a fast tune. *No matter how I feel or how much I'm attracted to Rafe Pierce, it's a lost cause.*

Chapter Twelve

Willow sat on a flat rock and watched the sun slowly sinking. Another day gone and Ash Hollow drew closer with the passing of each one. The extra six wagons had pulled away from them in the middle of the afternoon. Merry waved good-bye to her newly found little friends and sighed as only a disappointed little girl can do. Willow wondered if she herself would sigh like that when she watched Rafe ride away to the north after they'd gotten past Ash Hollow.

Pale pinks, bright reds, and every shade of orange in the Lord's palette mixed together to bring Willow a beautiful sunset to compensate for the gnawing sadness deep in her heart. Just as the last thin line of sun disappeared on the horizon, a rustle in the leaves behind her startled her, and she turned quickly to scan the scattered trees silhouetted in the pale moonlight. Her ears ached as she listened intently.

"Must be an animal," she mumbled, standing up and brushing the back of her skirt. Before she took a step she heard the whimper. It was barely more than a moan of anguish, but it was human. She rolled her eyes toward heaven. If Merry had coerced one of those little girls into going with them, Hank was going to have a genuine, un-adulterated hissy fit. Not to mention the child's mother and father. They'd have to return for her and no doubt Annie would have to punish Merry. The uplifted spirits among the women on the train after the social event the night before would be spoiled.

For a moment, Willow considered ignoring the second little sob. If Merry had talked some child into following the train, then someone else could discover the deed tomorrow. But the thought of a scared little girl out there in the darkness melted that idea, and she followed the slight noises until she came to a huge old oak tree. A child was curled up in a tight little ball at its base, her head on her drawn-up knees and her bony arms wrapped tightly around them, as if by not looking up the darkness would disappear.

Willow reached out and touched the child on the arm, and the little girl jerked her head up, the whites of her eyes shining in the darkness. "Merry?" Willow said.

"Oh, Miss Willow, I thought you was one of them. I hid but I was afraid they'd find me so I tried not to look." She threw herself into Willow's arms. "They'd kill me for sure, Miss Willow. One of them even said that there was a kid on the train who'd seen them so they couldn't tie up with this train."

"Whatever are you talking about, child?" Willow hugged her closely and stroked her head like she was a puppy. "Annie's going to be worried sick about you, honey. Let's go on back to camp."

"It was them, Miss Willow. They were right down there by the creek. I sneaked off to see where you was goin'. I know I ain't 'posed to make no trouble. But you sneak off at night and I just wanted to see if you was meeting Uncle Rafe. It was bad but please don't tell Uncle Hank. He'll be mad at me," Merry sobbed.

"Where are they now? And who are they?" Willow asked.

"They just now rode off. Said they'd have until daybreak to reach that other train. Oh, Miss Willow, they're going to kill all my friends just like they did my family. They said they'd probably do better with that train than trying to take some of our oxes. They're going to do it like they did my family, and I hid and it was so scary. They're going to ride easy 'til first light and then kill them. What are we going to do?" Merry looked up into Willow's face, sure of her adult wisdom.

"Well." Willow thought for a moment, her mind spinning so fast she felt dizzy. What to do? What to do? She could race into the men's camp and tell them what had happened and let them take care of it, but little Merry would be in trouble for breaking rules about going outside the camp after the day's end. And it would be all Willow's fault. Rafe would give her one of those "I told you so" looks and there would be another fight. Or she could take care of matters herself and no one would have to know a blessed thing. She could reach the six wagons by midnight and easily be back at her own train before daybreak. If the folks there had forewarning, they could take care of the problem. She only had to ring the warning bell; not stay and fight the battle. No one would even need to know she'd rode out. The only problem was a horse.

"We need to tell Uncle Rafe, don't we? And then Uncle Hank will know I was bad and the whole train will be in big trouble," Merry said.

"No, we don't need to tell anyone. You hurry on back to the camp and go to bed just like nothing happened. I'm going to ride out to that other train and tell the fiddler what has happened. If those men know what's going on then they can take care of it. If I'm not back by daybreak then you can tell your Uncle Rafe," Willow said. "Now you hurry back and curl up in your bed. And Merry, I wasn't meeting Rafe out here. I just happen to like the peace of a sunset. We'll take care of this and no one will have to know you were ever out of camp."

"Okay, Miss Willow, and I promise I won't break the rules no more." Merry ran as fast as she could back to Annie's wagon. She pulled the covers up over her head and prayed desperately that Willow would save all her little friends.

Willow jumped at every noise and for the first time wished her sisters would simply hush and go to sleep. Usually she loved the half hour after they were tucked into their bedrolls, when amid quiet whispers they got to know each other better. But that night she would have been content to hear them all snore as loudly as Connie did under the adjoining wagon.

Time wasn't a problem. The other train couldn't be more than six miles from them right now. Those worthless bandits would locate their prey and sleep the rest of the night before the attack. Which would not go the way they'd planned. She hoped the men who'd murdered everyone on Merry's little wagon train found themselves trussed up like Thanksgiving turkeys and brought to Ft. Kearny. The military men there could hang them and Willow swore if she was in the area, she'd watch without flinching.

Her skin itched with worry as she waited to be absolutely sure her four sisters were breathing softly in deep sleep. She inched away from them and into the wagon, where she opened her trunk, donned her overalls and flannel shirt, stuffed her feet into her boots, and picked up the six-shooter. She loaded it and quietly stepped out into the darkness. She'd borrow Rafe's horse for the trip because it knew her better than the other animals did. Luck was with her when she crept up to the line of horses. The big black beast nuzzled her hand after he'd eaten the sugar lump she offered and stood perfectly still while she saddled him. Although most of the men used their saddles as pillows, she'd overheard Rafe telling Hank that sleeping on a saddle gave him a pain in the neck. She mounted with ease and leaned over the horse's neck to whisper softly in his ear as she rode him away from the camp. Rafe would never know that she'd borrowed Buster. Not in a million years. And Merry wouldn't get into trouble, either.

The trail was easy to follow by the moonlight for the

first two hours, then suddenly it split. Willow swung down off the horse's back and bent down. Two sets of tracks. One going slightly north like she'd expect. The other veering off just a bit to the northwest. She walked a while, following the first set of tracks, sure that she was going the right way. She checked the moon. High up in the sky. She still had lots of time before daybreak so she walked a while longer to be absolutely sure. Then she saddled up and urged the horse into a trot. An hour later she saw the wagons circled up in the quietness of wide open space, sitting ducks for the killing spree about to take place. She scanned the area for the thinnest thread of tell-tale smoke from the evil men's campfire, but couldn't see a thing, so she carefully made her way to the five wagons. *Five?* She counted them a dozen times. There had been six, she was sure of it. Six wagons. Six big strong men and more than a dozen women with lots and lots of children. Then five or six more men who were there to scout and protect. Just like Baker, who for some crazy, strange reason had signed on with Hank to go as far as Independence Rock. Connie said she heard that he wanted to make a few dollars to help set up a home of his own when he got to Utah.

But what happened to the other wagon? Willow tightened her grip on the pistol as she rode up to the wagons. Everyone would probably be asleep, but she wasn't taking chances. She dismounted and tied the horse's reins to the back of a wagon, then stepped inside the camp. The embers of a fire glowed bright orange in the middle and a man snoozed with his chin propped up on a rifle.

Willow touched him lightly on the shoulder and he jerked awake in an instant. "Who are you?" He whipped the rifle up and sighted a spot right between the prettiest blue eyes he'd ever seen. "Why, you are a woman! What are you doing here?"

"Warning you, but where's the other wagon?" Willow asked.

"Warning me of what? And there's only five of our wagons. We're going a few miles northwest to homestead a few acres. Five of us brothers and our families," the man said. "What are you warning us of, lady?"

Willow's heart sank. She'd followed the wrong trail for more than an hour and now she'd have to ride hard to get to the other wagon train before daylight. "There's two bandits out there who are out to kill everyone and steal the wagons and livestock. They've done it before. We rescued a little girl who survived one of their attacks."

"Hey, you must be from that bride train. We heard about you from those folks going to Utah. Traveled along behind them for an hour or so today, then we split off and they went on. We'll be at our place by noon tomorrow . . . or is it today? Anyway, thanks for the warning. I'll wake up the rest of the train and we'll be prepared. Got any idea of how many of these killers is out there?"

"Two, far as I know," Willow said. "I've got to go, though, and warn the other train. That little girl I mentioned overheard them saying they'll strike at daybreak. You take care now, sir."

"You, too, little lady. And thanks for the warning." The man waved as she sped away on Buster's back.

Rafe Pierce is going to kill me, she thought miserably as she urged the horse into a run. *That is, if he doesn't hang me for horse thieving. Then he's going to give me those black looks until I shrivel up into nothing more than a bit of wind.*

"I don't care," she declared to stars and moon. "Let him act like a pompous cross-eyed donkey. I did what I had to do and I'll make it to those folks before daylight if I have to crawl. Faster, Buster," she urged the horse. "Rafe says you're the fastest thing on four legs. Honey, it's time to prove it. We might still make it back before daybreak if you can keep up this speed."

She made it back to the fork in the trail in a little less than an hour, dismounted, and made sure she was following the right set of tracks. From her calculations she still had plenty of time so she walked Buster for half an hour. Poor old boy had worked hard and needed at least a little consideration. When she slung her slim body back into the saddle she realized it was later than she'd originally thought. Dark clouds danced round the full moon and thunder rolled in the distance. There would be no sunrise that morning. The sweet smell of rain was in the air despite the ominous lightning and thunder. Doom. Willow's heart was a piece of stone, lying heavy in her chest. She could scarcely breathe. Would those horrid men strike early under the cover of a storm? No one would hear the repeat of a gun in a storm and everyone would be in the wagons. *Like sitting ducks for sure*, she thought. They could slaughter a wagonload at a time and the others would attribute the noise to nature's squall.

The dimness of a day trying to be born in the midst of a prairie lightning storm greeted Willow just as she saw the six little wagons circled up. She eased off Buster's back and watched for a few minutes. Something wasn't right, yet she couldn't put her finger on what it was. There were no gunshots and everything seemed peaceful. At least for a moment it did. Then screams filled the air. Goose bumps the size of the mountains in Mercersberg popped up on her arms, making every hair tingle with fear. Dread as cold as the icy mountain water of the stream on Aunt Harriet's farm raced down her backbone.

"Okay, you bunch of worthless farmers, wake up and smell the rain!" one of the men shouted so loud even Willow could hear it. "Come out of your wagons with your hands up. Send out the women and kids, too, or we'll shoot these two little blond-headed girls right between their eyes."

Men and women began pouring out from under the wagons, out of the backs and fronts, and even one lady hurried in to see what was the matter from outside the camp. *The fool*, Willow thought. *If she would've stayed out there she might've lived, like little Merry did. What would you have done if that would've been your child he was holding*? her conscience scolded.

"What do you want?" The fiddler asked nervously.

Willow jumped back into the saddle. They needed a diversion and by golly that's what they'd get. She hadn't ridden half the night to sit on her backside and watch all these nice people be murdered. Rafe Pierce might scream and yell like a wounded grizzly bear with an ingrown toenail, but she'd at least give her best to the job at hand.

"What do we want?" One of the men laughed. A mean, hateful sound, Willow thought as she decided which way she'd ride in from.

"Tell them what we want, Larry. Tell them we want all the supplies in those nice big fat wagons and we want their livestock. Two hundred head of cattle and a hundred sheep. Fort Kearny will pay us good for them. And the wagons will bring a fair price there, too." He pressed his pistol into the little girl's ear and she screamed.

"Take them," the fiddler said. "Take all of it but don't harm our children."

"We intend to take them," the man said. "Right after we make buzzard bait out of everyone on this train. Can't leave no witnesses what has seen our faces. You could turn us in in a hurry."

"And what do you intend to tell the soldiers at Fort Kearny?" the fiddler asked.

"That a little wagon train lost nearly all of its folks to an Indian raid and we bought out the rest of it. The leftover women and children latched onto another train going west. Wasn't but a couple of women and four or five brats. Works every time. Last time we took the booty back to St. Joe," the other man said, wrapping his hands around the little girl's braids and pulling her head back hard.

"Okay, boy, it's now or never," Willow whispered into Buster's ear, kicking him in the flanks at the same time. She rode in like a bat straight from the bowels of Hades, jumped the tongue between two wagons, and prayed the man didn't break the little girl's neck when she rode hell for leather right over the top of him.

The bandits turned just in time to see the big black monster of a horse coming right at them, but they didn't have time to do anything. One minute they were the big bad robbers, the next they were lying on the dirty ground, trying desperately to suck up some sultry Nebraska air into their deflated lungs. Two shots were fired when Buster plowed into the men with their cocked and ready pistols. One nicked Buster's ear and the other knocked Willow off his back.

One minute the wind was whipping through her unruly blond curls. She had her pistol in her hand to shoot either or both of the men if she had to. The next she was thrown from her horse's back, traveling halfway up to the clouds before she started to descend, like the rag doll Velvet had sewn for Merry. She thought about that doll and the pain in her chest as her body floated down, hitting the hard ground with a thud, and her spirit hovered upward to see what color the lightning really was.

"What in the devil do you think you are doing?" Rafe's voice sounded like it was right next to her ear. Great goodness, was he an angel who divided his time between heaven and earth?

"She's shot!" the fiddler yelled. "Mary, Sarah, Ruth, come and take care of this woman."

"No! No!" Rafe's screams pierced her ears. "I'll kill the sorry skunks."

"No, you won't," the fiddler said. "That's why we have the laws of the land. They will take care of these sorry skunks, as you so aptly say. Get them tied up, Hosea and Joshua. I don't care if they are injured from the horse's hooves. We'll take them into Fort Kearny and the military men can have them. Until then they get no help or attention. Tie them well and put them in my wagon. Hosea, you will ride with them into Fort Kearny today. Keep your gun well trained on them. Do you understand?"

"Yes, sir, I surely do." The older man nodded seriously. One of the little girls held hostage was his daughter. These two scoundrels would get no sympathy from him.

"Willow, wake up," Rafe whispered desperately into her ear.

"She's a brave woman," the fiddler said. "Came riding in here and right over the top of those men. Somehow the girls got loose and weren't harmed at all. The Lord rode with her, I'm sure. Malachi was wise to stay behind with your train to try to talk her into a marriage. She will make a fine first wife for him."

Willow opened one eye to see just exactly what heaven looked like and was surprised to see it was no different from Nebraska.

"Willow?" Rafe said gruffly.

She shut her eyes again. She hadn't died and Rafe Pierce had followed her. The reckoning was on its way and she was just too tired to deal with it. If she pretended to be dead, maybe he'd go away.

"Open your eyes, Willow," he demanded.

She breathed deeply, enjoying the simple pleasure of filling her lungs after having the wind knocked from her when she landed so hard on the baked earth. At first, she thought she'd never know that privilege again, when she figured she was dead and on her way out of this life. Men were everywhere at once, taking guns from the robbers and tying them up with ropes. When did Rafe get there? And why didn't he do something to stop them? Why did she have to do all the work?

"Willow?"

"Go away and leave me alone," she said without fluttering an eyelash.

"The gallus on her overalls deflected the bullet," a woman's voice said.

Willow felt soft hands checking the skin on her chest and something sticky and slightly warm oozing down under her arm.

"There's a scratch where the metal cut into her skin. I'll clean it and put a bandage on it, but if she's not harmed inside from that tremendous fall, she won't die from this gunshot wound," the lady said.

"Willow, wake up and tell me how you feel," Rafe demanded once again.

Her eyes popped open in spite of her reserve not to open them. "I feel like I've been thrown from the back of your horse. I feel like every muscle in my body is going to ache for days. I feel like shooting you. Why didn't you let me know you were out there?"

"Because I wasn't. I rode up just as you made that flying leap into the middle of this camp and caused all the fracas," he said. His arms ached to pick her up and hold her to his chest. She was alive. The blood wasn't from a deep heart wound.

"Just like a big-shot man. Arrive when the action is finished." She shut her eyes again.

"You're going to think the action has just begun," Rafe growled. "We've got to get on these horses and get back to our own train. I told Hank to go on. Make his fifteen miles all the way into Fort Kearny. Which means we make that many on horseback. So get up and stop playacting. You aren't dead, even though you may wish you were by the time we get to the fort."

"You are meaner than a rattlesnake," she hissed.

"Probably. But you'll be wanting to get back to your new love, Malachi Brubaker. I understand he's going to woo you and marry you. You'll make a fine first wife, I'm told," Rafe said.

Willow sat straight up and brushed the woman's hand from her wound. "I can fix this. It's just a scratch. Just bleeds a lot because of where it is," she said. "And Rafe Pierce, you better watch your mouth. If I'd wanted to be a first wife, I could've done that without traveling a month in a bouncing stagecoach, or going to California on a wagon train, either. At this point, I think Aunt Harriet was a prophet speaking the pure gospel when she said all a man was worth was the price of a bullet. And don't you worry about me. I could ride fifteen miles cross-eyed and standing on my head on that horse over there."

The lady giggled. Never before had she seen a woman stand up to a man like that. In her world women were revered and protected, but they didn't speak their minds. It was right next door to blasphemy and was surely a horrible sin.

Rafe glared at Willow. Ash Hollow couldn't come quick enough. Maybe, just maybe, if he was lucky, nothing else would happen between here and there. "Then let's ride," he said.

"Not without your breakfast," the lady said. "This wonderful woman has saved all of our lives this morning with her daring spirit. I will see to it you are both fed and we'll make a pack to send with you for the day's meals."

"I thank you," Willow said. A whole day alone on the trail with Rafe Pierce. Couldn't God have given her a better reward for her "daring spirit" than that? And what were they talking about her being Malachi Brubaker's first wife? She wasn't going to be any wife of that kid's. She'd rather reach the end of the journey and take her chances with some gold miner.

Chapter Thirteen

They rode in silence for more than an hour, each wallowing in their own steaming pot of fury. Black clouds hovered over them, but they weren't nearly as dark as Rafe's and Willow's moods. Thunder rumbled, but it wasn't as loud as their thoughts. Rain threatened, a few huge drops dotting the earth, but if they hit either Willow or Rafe they sizzled and evaporated in shared red-hot anger before either even felt the moisture.

Willow's chest ached. A big blue bruise was already forming around the thumbnail-sized scratch. Every bone in her body reminded her that they'd been abused as her horse kept a steady pace with Rafe and Buster. Her hair blew back into a tangled mess that would take her hours to comb out. Humidity coupled with just plain old hot wind made her skin so sticky that every particle of dust clung to her. Blast Rafe's soul to the devil. He cooed and promised Buster all kinds of fancy treats, telling him how sorry he was that poor old Buster had to go all the way to Fort Kearny with no rest. Well, what about Willow? She hadn't had any more rest than Buster and she looked twice as bad.

Rafe checked the nick in Buster's ear one more time. Another six inches to the right and the bullet would have got him right between the eyes. His ear would be mal-

141

formed, but it would take a trained eye to even notice the
tiny little snip, and besides, he had no intention of ever
getting rid of his favorite horse. When Buster was too old
to ride, he would turn him out to pasture to finish up his
last days. What on earth could Willow Dulan be thinking
anyway? Stealing his horse. Riding out to face two dangerous men like that. Didn't she have any idea of what a
woman's place was?

Oh, hush, his conscience admonished. *You were worried
sick about her. If you didn't love her so much you wouldn't
care what happened to her and you sure wouldn't be this
upset.*

Love her! he thought. *Love Willow Dulan? That's the
laugh of a lifetime.*

"Why'd you come after me?" Willow asked before he
had time to argue with that hateful inner voice telling him
things he didn't want to hear.

Rafe had to bite his tongue to keep his mouth from blurt-
ing out that he loved her. Now wouldn't that be a total
disaster after an already horrible experience. She'd throw
back her head and laugh louder than the ear-splitting thunder. Willow, with her spitfire attitude, could never love
Rafe Pierce. Besides, what was it that fiddler said about
Baker hiring on so he could court her? Well, he could have
Willow. He'd need more power than could even be harnessed in heaven if he expected to tame that wildcat. A
smile twitched the corners of Rafe's mouth when he
thought about the day Malachi Baker came in with another
woman, announcing that Willow had the ultimate honor of
being his first wife, but this little cutie was going to be the
second one, and maybe next year, if the crops were good,
he'd add a third. That should kindle a blaze big enough to
erase the whole state of Utah from the map.

"Did you wake up and find Buster gone or what?" she
asked when he didn't answer right away.

"It was my turn to ride guard for a couple of hours and
Buster wasn't there. I figured he'd broken the tether and so

I went looking around the camp for him. I found Merry Briley sitting beside their wagon crying her eyes out. She said you'd gone off and they were going to kill you with all the rest of her friends. I made her tell me what was going on and I went back to tell Hank. Borrowed one of the extra horses and you know the rest. It was a fool thing you did, Willow," he said.

"Yeah, well, it worked," she said.

"Hmpph!" He snorted and refused to say another word.

The clouds scattered sometime late in the morning, sending sunrays down in a glorious pattern, but Willow didn't even notice. Questions kept eating at her soul. Answers were as elusive as the clouds scuttling away to the northwest. When her brain felt as if it were going to explode, she swallowed her pride and asked Rafe what she considered safe questions. The ones concerning why her heart wouldn't behave around him would have to lie unanswered forever.

"Why are there so many women on that train and so few men? While I was watching I noticed at least two or three women claiming each wagon along with one man. What's going on there, Rafe?"

"That's the way those folks believe, Willow." He gave up the information grudgingly. Now he wouldn't have to watch the sky to the west every night and wonder if the state of the Utah was still intact or if Malachi had brought in another wife. His gut wrenched in a tight knot at the thought of that boy holding Willow in his arms and watching the sunset at the end of the day.

"Are you telling me that those men have more than one wife each?" she asked, her big blue eyes widening in wonder.

"That's what I'm telling you. They have as many wives as they can afford to support. The first wife does have a little more honor than the others. She usually takes care of more of the organization of the home. At least that's what I've been told." He'd give young Malachi that much help.

"And the women don't have a problem with that?" She cocked her head over to one side, trying to figure out if Rafe was telling her a tall tale and would laugh his fool head off at her later for believing it.

"They've been raised to believe that. It's in the Good Book, you know. God told those people to go forth and multiply. It says David had many wives. And remember the story about Jephthah? His father had seventy or eighty sons in addition to Jephthah, who was illegitimate. Well, those folks believe the Good Book down to the letter," Rafe said. "I've heard tell the women feel like they are sisters and raise their children all together. That's why there's more women than men. I'm surprised Malachi Brubaker didn't go on with them. Seems like he'd feel needed to protect his own."

"Gypsy said she heard he's making a little money so he can have his own place sooner. Guess he's already got a woman picked out to be his first wife," Willow said.

"Guess he does," Rafe said, a cold hard chunk of ice freezing the blood flowing in his veins. He shivered in spite of the heat and humidity.

They rested for the nooning beside a shallow creek running at the bottom of a six-foot cut through the countryside. Rafe dropped down the incline and lifted his hat filled with water up to Willow, who watered the horses. When they'd drunk their fill, she told Rafe she was coming down the side of the embankment to get her own water. She wasn't about to drink from his sweaty old hat.

Rafe had made it look so easy when he ground his boot heel into the soft dirt and walked down the slope to the clear bubbling little creek. Surely it wouldn't be that hard, she told herself as she put her small boot heel into the groove he'd left behind. She tested her weight gingerly against the soft earth and it held, giving her confidence.

Proving that she could do anything he could—and maybe some things even better.

Her foot missed the second hole and she gasped as she began to fall forward. It was the same feeling that she'd had when Buster bucked her off his back there at the camp. She braced herself for the thud and hoped she didn't break any bones this time.

Rafe did what came naturally; he took two steps forward and caught Willow. The silly woman was sure enough having a tough time that day. First she'd fallen off a horse and now down into the ditch. And there he was saving her sorry hide just to take her back to the wagon train for Malachi Brubaker to court. Somehow even in the twinkling of the eye that it took him to catch her it just didn't seem fair.

"Oh," Willow said when she realized she was in Rafe's arms, held so close to his chest she could hear his heart thumping. In her fear of falling, she locked her arms around his neck and held on for dear life. She should have wiggled her way clear and out of those strong arms but instead she looked right up into his eyes, only inches from her face.

Rafe couldn't take his eyes from those beautiful, strange-colored blue-green ones staring up at him. Fear of falling filled them to the brim, and yet there was something else, too. Something that tugged at his heartstrings and begged him to look even deeper into the soul of their owner, to discover what it was Willow Gail Dulan really wanted to do with her life.

He bent his head just slightly and she closed her eyes. His lips found hers and two wandering souls met there in the middle of Nebraska. At first it was a sweet kiss that only created a few sparks, then it deepened into something more, and somewhere off in the distance both of them heard something akin to church bells ringing.

Willow drew back reluctantly, wanting the kiss to go on, yet not ever wanting Rafe Pierce to know his touch on her arms, his mouth on hers, even the very gaze from his deep brown eyes could turn her into nothing more than a bowl of quivering clabber.

"Put me down," she said, her voice only slightly above a whisper.

"That wasn't very gentlemanly. I apologize for taking advantage of the situation," Rafe said.

So he was sorry he'd kissed her. She fought the urge to kick pure fire out of his shins. If her gun wasn't at the top of this six-foot ditch she'd have leveled it right at his heart and not even felt guilty when she pulled the trigger. God would understand and not even lay the charge to her sins, she figured, as she stood there trembling in rage and not able to expend one bit of it.

"Sorry? You're sorry you kissed me," she mumbled.

"No, I'm not sorry for the kiss. I'm sorry I took advantage of the situation," Rafe said.

"Sounds like you're splitting hairs to me," Willow said. "I'm going to get a drink and wash my face and then you can boost me back up. I'm going to eat my meal and sleep for thirty minutes before we go on. And Rafe, I don't accept your apology. I liked the kiss even if I don't like you."

He was speechless. Ladies didn't admit things like that. But then maybe he was splitting hairs, because to describe Willow as a lady was sure enough using the term very loosely.

By mid-afternoon it was evident another storm was brewing, approaching from the southeast and boiling up a good bit of rain, if the thunder and lightning were any indication of what was in store. Rafe kept an eye trained for any kind of shelter they could beg, buy, borrow, or steal. By his calculations they were six miles from Ft. Kearny, which should have been no problem, except for the ominous black clouds which were hollering amid the thunder that they were definitely going to be much later than supper time in getting to the fort.

When he'd just about given up on finding even a big,

hollow log to put Willow inside, he spied an old homestead. The stone chimney still stood, a lone sentinel of days when a family romped through the house. Rafe scanned the area around the blackened remains of the house. A small cemetery with wooden crosses marking the end of lifetimes on a hill shaded by two big oak trees. An outhouse, but the roof was gone. Some fallen-down fence lines around where a barn used to stand. And some grass growing over the door of a root cellar.

"A root cellar," Rafe yelled over the din of the storm, coming on fast by then, the first big drops of rain already splattering in the dusty ground.

"I'm not going in no abandoned root cellar," Willow said. "Besides, we can't put the horses in there."

"I'll tether them to the outhouse door. That should be safe enough," he shouted as he slid off Buster's back and led him in that direction. Willow sat still. Spiders lived in root cellars. She was so tired from being awake for more than thirty hours that she envisioned spiders as big as ground hogs living in there, just waiting to pounce on her when she opened the door. No, Willow was not going into that root cellar. Rafe Pierce could ride one of those bicycle things on a barbed wire fence, sing her favorite song, and hand her a fistful of roses and she still wouldn't follow him into a root cellar.

"I'm not going in that hole!" she shouted.

"Oh yes you are," Rafe declared. He took the horse's reins from her hands and led him to the outhouse, wrapping the leather strips around the door handle several times.

Willow didn't budge.

"You could be hit by lightning, Willow. Get off that horse and come on." He held up a hand to help her dismount.

She folded her arms across her chest and shook her head.

Rafe didn't have time to plead with the woman. She'd ridden a horse into the middle of a band of thieves, so what was her problem? Come to think of it, she'd jumped into a raging river to save his life when there was danger of snakes all around her. She didn't have an ounce of fear in her.

"Willow, I'm not playing games with you," he said.

She turned her head and refused to look at him.

He reached up and with one swoop, picked her off the horse as deftly as if he'd been picking ripe apples from the trees on his ranch. "Yes, we are going to that cellar," he said, draping her over his shoulder like a bag of chicken feed.

She beat on his back with her fists and called him every ugly, mean word she could find in her vocabulary. One minute he was a disgusting swine, the next a devil in disguise, but when he opened the door to that black hole with no light, he became a heartless, brainless fool.

"If you move or start back up those stairs, I'll hog tie you," Rafe said without an ounce of warmth in his deep voice. "Here's a bit of tallow candle left behind so we'll have a little light. I'm going to set you down and shut this door, Willow. You'd better be good."

Her jaw hurt, she set it so tightly. She wouldn't speak to him, she decided as she surveyed the inside of the cellar, looking for the monstrous spiders lurking in the corners. If she saw one, she'd be halfway to Ft. Kearny before Rafe got that little chunk of tallow lit, and that was a pure fact.

"Cozy," he said, looking around. It was empty except for the tallow candle set on an upturned milk bucket with a hole in the bottom. No food, no chairs, just an old mattress in the corner filled with corn shucks. At least it was warm and dry and they could wait out the storm there. Surely in an hour or so it would be past and they could still make the fort before dark.

"Pick that mattress up," she said, pointing to the corner.

"Why?"

"Because," she said simply.

She was slap-silly. Lack of sleep had her seeing booger bears everywhere, Rafe decided. He picked up the mattress and shook it firmly. Not one baby mouse ran out, but then he could have told her there was nothing inside the place. There was no food, and even a simple house mouse had to have food.

She looked under the thing and all around it. By the time he had it back on the dirt floor, she had her boots off.

"What are you doing?" he asked.

"I'm going to sleep. You can wake me when this storm is over. I was so tired I couldn't sleep at nooning. But I can now. If I don't get some rest I'm going to fall off that horse out there." She lay down on the mattress and shut her eyes.

Rafe listened to the hard rain, coupled with small hail stones, beating on the cellar door, and watched Willow's chest rise and fall as she breathed in and out, deep in sleep. The cellar was less than six feet tall so he had to stoop, and his shoulders began to ache. The mattress was wide enough he could take the backside and never touch Willow. At least he could stretch out his bones a while. He'd been running on sheer, raw nerves as long as Willow had.

He pulled off his boots and eased his weary body down on the mattress, careful not to touch or wake Willow. A feather bed with fresh, line-dried sheets in the springtime had never felt so good. He turned his back to Willow and pulled one knee up, slipped his hands together under his cheek for a pillow, and shut his eyes. He wouldn't really go to sleep, just rest his eyes for a little while.

Willow wiggled and sighed. She flipped over on her side and threw her arm across the extra pillow she always used in her feather bed at Aunt Harriet's. One pillow to put under her head, one to hold.

Rafe didn't know when she cuddled up to his back. He was already in a sleep every bit as deep as what Willow was enjoying.

Chapter Fourteen

The candle had long since burned itself out when Rafe awoke with a start, wondering in the pitch-black darkness where he was. By the time he got his eyes fully open and slipped out of Willow's embrace, he knew exactly where he was and why he was there. He felt along the packed dirt sides of the cellar and found the stairs. Everything sounded quiet out there. The storm must have passed while he napped. He threw open the door to the most glorious sunrise he'd seen in days.

Rafe's heavy black eyebrows knitted together into a solid line at the base of a forehead full of wrinkles as he tried to wake up. Something was terribly wrong. The sun did not set in the east. Was he turned around completely? If that was the case, then where was Ft. Kearny?

It's a sunrise, his conscience said bluntly. *You have slept through the night.*

He moaned. Now what would he do? Marry Willow Dulan because he'd compromised her reputation? Hank was going to hang him from the nearest scrub oak tree.

Rays of light filtering through the curtains in Willow's old bedroom awakened her. She stretched without opening her eyes. What would this Sunday bring? Would Pete surprise her with an unexpected visit?

150

"Willow, wake up." Rafe's hoarse voice jerked her back into reality.

She sat up and rubbed her eyes, as reality replaced a fuzzy dream world. "Did the storm pass?"

"I guess it did. Sometime yesterday," he said gruffly. Buster wasn't tied to the outhouse door anymore. Neither was the spare horse.

"Don't tease me, Rafe," Willow said, wishing for a cup of strong, black coffee to take the taste of hard sleep from her mouth.

"I'm not teasing. I lay down on the back side of that mattress with you and it appears we slept right through the night. And to top it all off, I don't see Buster or your horse," he said.

She grabbed her boots, jumping around on one foot as she put them on and tried to climb the rickety stairs at the same time. She had a vague recollection of cuddling up to her extra feather pillow several times, wrapping her arms around it and snuggling down into warmth. High color filled her cheeks as she realized just who that pillow had been. Hopefully, Rafe had been sleeping soundly and didn't even know she was wrapped around him. It was a blessed wonder that a red-hot blaze didn't ignite from her face when she remembered throwing a leg over her pillow.

"We didn't really sleep through the night?" she gasped when she looked out at the bright new morning dawning on a cloudless day.

"Yes, we did," he said. He put a finger in the corner of his mouth and whistled shrilly enough to make Willow grab her ears.

Buster appeared from a grove of trees back behind where the barn had stood. He trotted over to Rafe and nuzzled his ear. In a moment the other horse ambled over to Buster and waited. Rafe could have kissed both of the animals on their bewhiskered mouths, he was so relieved. Six miles was enough of a journey on horseback, but if they'd had to walk it would have taken all morning.

"Rafe, what are we going to do?" Willow asked.

"We're going to mount these horses and ride like the devil to Fort Kearny. We'll stop there for a quick meal and then go on. I don't think for one minute that Hank is sitting there waiting for us. He'll go right on as planned. Maybe we'll catch them by evening or before if there's no more summer storms," he said, already in the saddle by the time he'd finished the last word.

"I'm thirsty and I'm hungry," she said as she slipped a foot into the stirrup and sat down in the semi-wet saddle with a thud.

"Well, honey, you got a choice. You can ride that horse to the wagon train, or you can take that little pop gun you carry, shoot him between the eyes, and have a big old horse steak for breakfast this morning," Rafe said.

"I understand why some folks are cannibals," Willow retorted. "Bet that one day a wife got tired of her husband having a hateful mouth and she just shot him, put him in the boiling pot, and fed the whole tribe with his sorry hide."

"Probably the other way around. He shot her for her mean mouth, put her in the boiling pot, fed the whole tribe, and then they all died of food poisoning," he came right back at her. He urged Buster into something between a trot and an all-out run. She could keep up or stay behind and eat her horse. Right then Rafe's whole world was in confusion. Would Hank tell him to marry this snippet, or would he be glad to see his old friend still alive and well? Did Rafe really love Willow or was it just some kind of strange physical attraction because she had blond hair and those fascinating eyes? The fresh morning wind whipping across his unshaven cheeks had no answers.

Willow kneed her horse into a run and kept a steady pace with Buster. Of all the luck. She'd bedded down with a man, but they'd slept like the dead, they were so tired. Great Scott! She wouldn't really come to bed in dirty overalls, with her hair uncombed, her face unwashed for two days, and her body smelling like something between a dead skunk and Aunt Harriet's outhouse in the summertime. Gypsy might tease her, but when she told them what the conditions were, they'd understand. No one would really expect her to marry up with Rafe Pierce just because she spent the night with him.

Marry Rafe? her mind shouted above the thunder of the horse's hooves. Now that was a real laugh, but what if Connie caused a big stink about her not being fit for a husband in Bryte? Well, that might be her salvation after all. She couldn't marry a man because she was tainted goods.

They ate a hasty meal with General Hodges at the fort in the middle of the morning. The two murderers were in custody. Merry Briley had identified them both when the wagon train stopped an hour for supplies. Mrs. Hodges was kind enough to give Willow a handful of pins and a comb to tidy up her hair, along with a basin of water to wash her face and hands. The general informed them that the train had indeed gone on at daybreak, with the message left behind that Hank intended to make only ten miles that day. With any luck, Willow and Rafe should catch them right about nooning or a little past that.

Luck finally did kiss them both and they caught sight of the train while it paused for nooning. They hadn't spoken a word for more than an hour when they rode up to the last wagon, where all four of her sisters waited to smother her with hugs and questions. Rafe ignored them all and rode on to the small group of men a few hundred feet from the train.

"So what happened?" Gypsy finally asked the question on all their minds.

"We saved the other train. I kicked Rafe's old horse in the flanks and rode into the middle of the two men. Got shot but my overalls' gallus deflected the bullet. Rafe came right in behind me, I guess. I was knocked out cold but the fiddler and his men had already taken control of the murderers. Anyway, then we came back," she said.

"And?" Velvet raised an eyebrow. "We'd given you up for dead, along with Rafe Pierce. You should've been back by last night, easily. What happened?"

"We got caught in that storm and holed up in an old abandoned root cellar," Willow said, trying to sound very uncaring about the whole situation. "I'm dirty and hungry. Think I could have a basin of water and a few minutes to change out of these horrible sweaty clothes?"

"Ladies don't sweat. They perspire," Velvet said.

"Then I ain't a lady," Willow said.

"I got a question," Garnet said. "We stopped for the storm. Lasted one hour. That leaves about twenty-eight or more uncounted for. Want to explain about those?"

"No, I do not," Willow said. "Trust me. Nothing happened. I trust you when you tell me you played a piano in a saloon and nothing happened. So now you got to trust me."

"Fair enough," Garnet said.

"Guess we'll have to have a hair-pulling, biting fight with Connie," Gussie laughed. "Little sister says she's innocent of anything unmoral, then she's innocent. Connie might not see it that way and it'll be a real shame to have to whoop her hind end sometime before the end of the day."

"Lord, Almighty, I shall be glad to see Ash Hollow and the last of Rafe Pierce." Willow rolled her eyes toward heaven. "We fell asleep in the root cellar. We'd missed a whole night's rest and were exhausted and it was dark. When we awoke, it was daylight. We rode like the devil to get here this early. Now I'm going to wash up. If Connie says one word, you four stand out of the way and I'll take care of it. I'd gladly whoop someone right now just to get all this rage out of my soul." Willow wasn't about to admit she'd actually slept with Rafe, all tangled up around his hard, muscular body just like a wanton saloon hussy.

"Deal." Velvet grinned. So her little sister was riding

along on an emotional stagecoach with a busted wheel and a road filled with pits. Velvet took her place in the driver's seat and was careful to keep it slow while Willow changed into clean clothing. However, there wouldn't be a fight with Connie. Velvet would see to that.

They passed Platte Crossing, with its desert swamp of a river. Willow figured it must be at least half a mile wide, maybe even wider, and about an inch deep. Calling it a river was as accurate as calling Rafe Pierce a gentleman. Any other man would have at least made the offer to marry her after sleeping with her all night. But not Rafe. He'd scarcely spoken to her since they returned from the save-the-other-wagon-train escapade. Tipped his hat most mornings to them as a group and merely said, "Ladies," as he rode on, staying just far enough ahead or behind their wagon so talk wasn't even an option.

Willow was glad he hadn't followed her to watch her beloved sunsets in the evenings. She was glad she could just sit there in silence and not even think of a week ago when she and Rafe shared that kiss at the bottom of the ravine where such good clean water ran freely in that little creek. She pulled her knees up and wrapped her arms around them, watching the day end on the horizon in a blaze of glory.

"Sunsets," she mumbled. "They're the only thing a woman can depend on. They're a living, pulsating spirit that holds the promise of the true promised land out there beyond it somewhere."

"I agree," a masculine voice said right at her elbow.

"You startled me," she said, her heart falling somewhere down farther than even the soles of her boots.

"I'm so sorry," he said. "I saw you ease out away from the circle and followed you tonight. Been meanin' to speak to you for a long time, Willow Dulan. You see, I've a mind to marry you."

She looked at him as if he'd grown two extra ears. Surely

her mind was playing tricks on her. No one just spit out a proposal like that. Menfolks wooed and courted and then proposed.

"You going to answer me?" he asked.

"No, Mr. Malachi Brubaker, I don't think I am," she said, shifting her body away from him so there was more distance between them.

"I didn't expect you would, Willow. Not right here at the first. It's probably a shock to hear me say that. Especially after that business with Rafe Pierce. But I overheard him telling Hank all about it and way I see it your reputation is ruined, but my people won't know that. They'll just see you as some kind of savior who kept them from being killed. That'll go a long way to rectify the fact you ain't one of us yet. But you will be. Soon as we can get the words said and your name on the book. I'll be right good to you and never bring it up that you were tainted goods when I got you. I've had a hankering for you ever since I first laid eyes on you that night, so I'm offering you a decent name and the honor of being my first wife. Rafe said he told you about how my people believe so you understand what I'm saying. It's really not so bad once you give it some thought. The women share the work so you won't be old and worn-out by the time you are fifty years old. You can think on it a while. By the time we get to Independence Rock, you might see the light," he said, quickly reaching across the distance between them to kiss her on the cheek.

She wiped it away. "Don't hold your breath, Mr. Brubaker. I'm not going to be anyone's first wife, not unless I die real early and my husband finds another woman. I don't hold no hard feelings about your belief. Everyone is entitled to think what they want to. We fought a war so we could do just that in this country. I'm not interested in marrying anyone, and I won't ever share my husband with another woman. I already passed up an opportunity like that, so good night." Willow stood up and walked away from him.

He smiled at her swaying hips. She'd change her mind. By Independence Rock she'd change it. Already some of the women were shunning her, especially that shrew, Connie, bless her heart. Rafe Pierce would be gone after Ash Hollow and Baker figured he'd keep Connie fed with the right information about what really went on out there when he and Willow left the campsite at night: she'd take care of the rest for him. Yes, Willow Dulan would be glad to marry him at Independence Rock. She'd make a fine first wife. He whistled as he went back to camp. And she wouldn't have time to waste time watching some silly sunset in the evenings, either. He'd take care of all her evening hours.

Rafe watched Willow stomp back into the circle, then in a few minutes Baker appeared from the same area. He had a springy step and his whistling filled the night air. So the courting had begun. Well, power to the kid. Even if Rafe's crazy heart kept telling him he had fallen in love with the woman, he'd overcome it. Just like he did the time before. Willow Dulan wasn't the woman for him, and he'd have his hide tacked to the smokehouse door before he ever admitted that he was even vaguely attracted to her, much less hopelessly in love with the spitfire hellcat.

"So did young Baker declare his intentions?" Velvet asked Willow when they'd all bedded down for the night.

"How'd you know?" Willow whispered.

"He's been busy as an old woman at a quilting bee," Velvet said. "Spinning his threads in all the right directions. He's bound to have you, you know."

"Well, it does sound like a wonderful idea. Lots of wives so the work is divided amongst us. Wouldn't have to look at a man's sorry old face every morning. Just every now and then when I drew the unlucky straw," Willow teased.

"Sure thing. I can just see you in that situation without

a bit of jealousy," Gypsy snorted. "All Connie has to do is flit around Rafe, and you're green."

"Hush, I'm going to sleep," Willow declared. "And you are wrong. Connie can have Rafe Pierce. Matter of fact, I wish she would rope him and brand him for her own."

"Then maybe you think you could get over him," Gypsy said. "It don't work that way. Hey, why don't you tell us about that root cellar?"

"Why don't you all go to sleep?" Willow pounded her pillow. Love Rafe enough to be jealous? Good grief! That was a joke.

She was still awake long after midnight, trying to make sense of the whole thing. Maybe she should change her way of thinking and marry Baker. Those men did seem to be proud of their wives and almighty good to them.

No, that wasn't the answer. She'd just go on to Bryte, and take her chances that there would be a hundred women who really wanted husbands. Before she fell asleep, Willow figured she might actually be cut out to be an old maid. Men were just too much trouble.

Chapter Fifteen

Ash Hollow was a lovely valley where the wagon train would strike the Sweet River, once they got down to it, that was. All the women were excited about having a real bath and good sweet water when they got to the bottom of the bluffs towering up on either side, some 60 feet high. Willow looked at the wild flowers growing along with small cedars and scrub ash in the crevices down the side of the bluffs and shuddered. More than twenty wagons, all the horses, oxen, and women to crawl down that steep incline. Suddenly that little ten foot drop to the creek on the journey she shared with Rafe last week looked almighty small.

"We'll all be killed," Connie whined. She shivered at the idea of what the wagon train had to do. "We've come all this way Rafe, only to die. There's no way I can get down those rocks, let alone all these wagons. You'll just have to help me, Rafe. Promise you'll hold my hand the whole way?"

"It's simple," Willow said before Rafe could answer. "We'll rough-lock the hind wheels, fasten a big rope to the axle of the wagon and all these big strong men will hold on to the rope to keep the wagon from going end over end. A couple of us women will steer it with the tongue and a few more can be on hand to ease it down the steps. If you look, it's solid rock steps right down there—see. They're about six inches to two feet apart, but that's not so far that the oxen can't manage or that we can't step it off either. Especially if we tie up our skirt tails with a length of rope so we don't get tangled up in them. It'll take all day. We can take the first brace of oxen down, then the women who belong to that wagon can walk down, right slowly. After that we'll take the last of the oxen for that wagon. Then will come the wagon and the women can get it rehitched and take care of anything that got shifted around inside."

"Pretty smart, Willow," Hank said. "You sure you never went on the trail with your dad when you were just a kid? You figured this out right quick. That is exactly the way we're going to do it. Your wagon won't go until the very end. Maybe not until tomorrow even."

"You know I didn't, Hank, but thank you. At least some folks think I can do something right. If we don't have a smash up, I bet we can get them all down today. It's barely daybreak," she said and smiled at him.

Rafe wished for a smile like that for his very own. If they really did get all the wagons safely into the Hollow and beside that beautiful river, then he could be at his ranch tomorrow night. He'd like to at least take one of those smiles with him. He chastised himself for even caring.

"Stop your carrying on Connie," he said in his gruffest voice. "You can sit right here and watch. By the time it's your turn, you'll be so bored you'll be eager to dance down those steps. Okay, first wagon, unhitch the oxen," he called out. "Which one of you is going to volunteer to lead them down?

"I'll do it," Willow said. "I'm not afraid of heights. Once I'm halfway down, let the first five girls start down. Give me five minutes to go put on my overalls. I'm not taking oxen in a dress."

Rafe rolled his eyes. It made more sense than a skirt, petticoats, and a parasol, but he didn't have to like it.

"Don't you look at me like that either, Rafe Pierce. I'm not about to fall to the bottom of that mess, and the way I figure it I'll make about fifty trips up and down today, so I'm wearing overalls." Willow pointed her finger at him.

"Not that it matters what you look like anyway," Connie snapped. "Wouldn't matter if you took the oxen down bare-butt naked. It's not like Rafe and probably several other men in this train hasn't already seen you that way."

Willow turned quickly to see Connie sneering and several other women giggling behind their fingertips. "Darlin', don't be judging me. I haven't got time to teach you some manners right now, but when the last wagon reaches the creek, you just remember, you've got a hard lesson to learn. It might not come tonight or even tomorrow. But it'll come before we reach Bryte, California, sweetie. So watch your back and your tongue. Now, Rafe, I'm going to change my clothes. I'll take all these oxen down today. One set at a time, and then I'll work on the horses. Like I said back in St. Joe, I'm a passable animal doc. They seem to trust me more than some people I know."

At noon half the wagons were in Ash Hollow. Willow had met Rafe and Baker easing the wagons down each time she climbed back up the irregular steps to claim another brace of animals. Every time they passed, her with oxen or without, him holding onto the back of a wagon or ascending to help with another one, their eyes met and held for a moment. Souls begging for uniting, hearts pleading for love—minds refusing both.

Willow grabbed a quick cold biscuit and downed a quart of cold, black coffee at nooning and went back to work. By mid-afternoon her hands had begun to cramp and her legs were little more than jelly on sticks. She remembered lots of afternoons when she'd felt that way on the farm. She and Aunt Harriet would get so tired, they'd be crazy, giggling like schoolgirls. But they'd simply kept moving and kept working, so she drew on her past reserve and kept working with the easygoing oxen.

At dusk there were two wagons left. The one Connie and Annie occupied with three other women, and the Dulan sisters' rig. Connie turned up her nose when Willow took the first brace of oxen down and came back for the second one.

"Okay, ladies," Willow said breathlessly. "It's your turn. Here's your ropes. You've seen the other women tie their skirts up to their knees. It'll keep you from tangling up and falling."

"Oh, yes, the smart Willow Dulan," Connie snipped. "Show all the men our legs so you won't be the only one who's a wanton woman."

Willow thought she'd had the whole situation with the shrew in control. But she hadn't banked on how tiring it really was to climb up and down those rocks. She wanted to be sitting in the middle of Sweet River with good, cold, clean water flowing over her sweaty skin. She wanted to watch the sunset one more time, knowing Rafe was close by, because tomorrow he would be gone.

"I think that's enough." Gypsy saw the glint in Willow's eye and started to step between the two women. "Connie, you'd best hush."

"I'll say whatever I want. I'm not afraid of a sawed-off woman in men's clothing," Connie said, pushing Gypsy aside with enough force to land her on her bottom at the very edge of the cliffs.

Willow opened her hand, took one step forward, and caught Connie right across her right cheek. Annie caught her before she hit the ground, stood her up, and slapped fire into her left cheek before she could catch her breath. "You will shut your sorry mouth, Connie, or I'll slap you again. Willow has worked all day and all you've done is whine. If she don't knock some sense into you then I'm going to. Is that understood?"

Tears streamed down Connie's face. She stormed away to the back of her wagon, threw herself down on the grass and seethed.

"She's got one coming from me," Gypsy said, dusting off her skirts. She'd been down the cliffs herself several times that day, steering the tongues of the wagons, and like Annie said, all Connie had done was whine, whine, whine—and flirt with Rafe Pierce.

"What's going on here?" Rafe said, peeping over the top of the rocks, coming up for one more wagon.

"Not a thing," Annie said.

"Nothing, 'cept Connie was ugly to Willow again so Willow slapped her and then Annie slapped her again," Merry said stoically. "But I just watched, Uncle Rafe. I didn't hit nobody, but Connie is pouting. She says you have to hold her hand all the way down the rocks. But I don't need you to hold my hand. I'm a big girl."

Rafe and Hank both clamped their jaws shut and held the laughter inside. So the first real catfight had just taken place and they'd missed it. Somehow, after the day's hard work, it didn't seem fair.

"Okay, ladies." Willow ignored Connie. "Let me get halfway down with this last set of oxen, and then you follow me. Your wagon will come after that and you can get everything hitched up to make the circle a few yards up the meadow beside the creek."

Willow coaxed the oxen with a soft voice, promising them lots of nice green grass if they'd just take one more step. Then another and another. They found their footing and slowly, slowly went down the incline. She'd just gotten them to the bottom and reunited them with their other two friends when she heard a slight whimper and looked up. Surely brave little Merry Briley wasn't having a last minute change of heart. The sight was completely surreal. One minute, Connie was picking her way gingerly down the steps; the next she stumbled over her untied skirt and tried to catch herself by flailing her hands out away from her body.

Willow would wonder in her later years how she managed to get fifteen feet up those rocks before Connie's hind end hit the first bump on the way to a bloody end, possibly with several broken bones to boot. She supposed it was because she'd climbed down so often that day, she knew exactly where the steps were and how far apart they were. One moment she heard the whimper, the next she was scaling the sheer wall like a mountain goat, another and she had Connie around the waist, holding her with all the strength left in her sinewy muscles.

"Don't you touch me. You ain't no better than one of the loose saloon women." Connie tried to push her backwards.

"One more time, darlin', and I'll step to the side and push you down this mess. Now, why didn't you tie up your skirts? Are you crazy or just plain stupid?" Willow screamed.

Rafe and Hank watched from the top. So they hadn't missed out on all the fun. The Dulan sisters had their skirts tied up, so they simply started walking down. All of them had made the trip in one capacity or another that day, so they didn't even need to look at where to step. Willow wasn't going to fight this one alone. No, blood was thicker than water, and Dulan blood was going to stand together. Connie was either going to learn her lesson and shut her sorry whining, belittling mouth or they'd whip some sense into her. If Hank had a problem with that then the Dulan sisters would wave good-bye to all their newly made friends and walk to the nearest town. Gypsy led the pack and looked forward to throwing that piece of uppity woman the rest of the way down the mountain. If the fall didn't kill her, then she'd drag her by all that blond hair to the creek and hold her under the water until the bubbles stopped coming up.

"You want this fight up here, or you want to drag those flowing skirts to the bottom?" Willow whispered.

"I don't want a fight at all," Connie whimpered. "I just want to get to the bottom and I want a bath."

"Then I would suggest you bite holes in your tongue

from now on." Gypsy grabbed her by the arm. "That's the rules from here to California, lady. Or else there'll be one disappointed gold miner at the end of this journey."

"Don't you threaten me, you half-Mexican fool." Connie tried to regain her bluff.

"Threaten?" Velvet said. "Who's threatening you, honey? We're statin' facts. Now, come along, we've come to help you down the cliffs. I'm taking one arm. Gussie will take the other. Willow is going before us and Garnet and Gypsy behind. One smart word and Willow is going to step out of the way and Gypsy is going to kick you into next week. And I'm sure you'll have the pick of the lot when we get to California because you'll be the only one who never showed your drawers."

The five Dulan sisters surrounded Connie and led her down the embankment like a silly child. All the way down they whispered to the woman, and at the bottom, merely turned and started back up to help get things ready for their own supplies to come down.

"Well, I'll be hanged," Rafe said when they reached the top. "I would've sworn you were all going to toss her to the lions rather than help her pick her footing."

"Looks can sometimes be deceiving, and you've got a problem along those lines." Willow tucked her chin down and looked up at him over the top of a sweat-stained, dirt-smudged face. "If I remember right, you didn't think the Dulan girls were made of stiff enough fabric to make this trip. You need to stop relying on first impressions, Rafe. Now let's get these last four oxen down there. I'm tired and hungry enough to eat a whole steer: hooves, bellow, and tail."

"Yes, ma'am." Rafe saluted smartly. "You are a fine drill sergeant. I'm surprised they didn't recruit you into the army."

She didn't intend to push him that hard. Not really, and she didn't realize he was standing so close to the edge. His arms went out to his sides like the wings of a great eagle and it looked like he might fly up and away to the puffy white clouds dotting the clear blue skies. *Maybe he was an angel after all and about to prove his meddle*, she thought in the split second it took her to reach out, grab his arm, and jerk him forward. The motion brought Rafe back to firm earth but the momentum brought him crashing down on top of Willow in the rut-worn earth.

Gypsy was the first one to giggle, then it became a full-fledged roar as the other sisters joined her, along with Hank and Bobby. Thank goodness that wicked Connie was already on the bottom and couldn't see Rafe sprawled out on top of Willow, Gypsy thought. She'd either have an apoplexy right there or else her big mouth would get her into more trouble than her tiny hind end could get her out of.

"Stop laughing." Willow rolled him off her body and tried to refill her lungs with the hot evening air. "It's not funny."

"Depends on whether you are under Rafe Pierce or standing off to one side watching him try to fly and you intent on keeping him grounded," Gussie said between giggles.

"You could have killed me," Rafe said through raspy, ragged breaths.

"If I'd wanted you dead, you'd be dead." Willow stood up and brushed off the seat of her filthy overalls. "Show's over, folks. Let's get the rest of this down so I can have a bath. I've had about all I can stand for one day."

Hank pulled a red handkerchief from the bib of his overalls and wiped the tears from his eyes. One more wagon and they'd make it to the bottom with no casualties. It was a sheer miracle, and her name was Willow Dulan.

Chapter Sixteen

The hardest thing Rafe Pierce ever did was walk away from the wagon train the next morning. Merry Briley was sobbing into her dress, her little bloomers shining for all the world to see. More than a hundred people waved good-bye as he climbed the rocks one more time to where Buster waited for him. He looked down, hoping to see Willow right behind him, scaling the incline. If she felt the way he did, there was no way she'd let him ride off without saying a single word. Evidently, she didn't.

Willow's heart was a chunk of stone, lying in her chest in an aching, throbbing, fierce pain. She had more love in her little finger for Rafe than he had in his whole body for her, or else he couldn't have turned his back and walked away. She'd get over it, she resolved with a toss of her head. She'd gotten over the measles when she was younger. It took ten days of lying in a darkened room with not a blessed thing to do, but she'd survived. In ten days, she vowed she'd be over Rafe Pierce. Miserable measles. Egotistical male. One and the same. She would survive.

"Let's move 'em out," Hank shouted. "Got a beautiful ride today, ladies, and more of Sweet River water tonight. Oh, and before we roll, let me introduce you to the fellow who's taking Rafe's place bringing up the rear end of the

167

wagon train. This is Pat O'Leary. We was expectin' Tavish O'Leary, but he's sent his uncle to do his job until we get to Independence Rock. Pat will be with us until then. Now let's get this show on the road, ladies."

Pat O'Leary had a full head of black hair that he parted on the side. His blue eyes were bedded down in a face full of wrinkles. His smile was genuine and kind, showing off a mouth full of straight white teeth that looked out of place with his age. He was sixty if he was a day, and Hank breathed a sigh of relief. At least he wouldn't lose a bride to him; even Connie had wrinkled her delicate little nose when she saw who was taking Rafe's place.

"Well, lookee here," Pat said, looking at Merry Briley from the top of his monstrous horse. "I believe you are too young to be marrying up just yet."

"Oh, Mr. O'Leary, I'm not going to Californee to get a husband. I'm going to get Annie a husband and me a daddy," she giggled.

"I believe that's Uncle Pat to you, young lady," Pat said. "Now give me your hand. I reckon that Irish here won't mind a little extra weight this mornin', and it's just not like Patty O'Leary to watch a pretty lass like you walk."

"Can I, Annie?" Merry asked, a smile on her face still streaked with tears from telling Rafe good-bye.

"Sure, child, just don't talk Mr. O'Leary's ears off this mornin'," Annie said.

"To be sure, ma'am, 'twill be the other way around. I'll talk her ears off. 'Tis the way of the Irish, you know. Only person who's kissed the Blarney Stone more times than old Patty O'Leary is my nephew, Tavish. Now there's a boy who could talk a priest into committing bank robbery. I'm thankin' you for sharing this precious child with me today," he said, tipping his wide-brimmed hat toward Annie.

Willow hitched up her skirts and took her place in the wagon seat. According to Rafe, his ranch was about twelve miles to the north of Ash Hollow. He'd be there with his sister, Katy, by nightfall. Would he ever think of her again?

Willow doubted it. She'd just be a faint memory in his mind by noon; by the time the sun set in the west tonight even that would be gone. She picked up the reins and wound them through her gloved fingers.

So be it. Ten days. That's what it would take to flush him out of her heart.

"Mornin', Miss Willow." Baker reached up from the back of his horse to touch her arm. "Guess you're glad to see that rapscallion on his way. It's a shame the way he ruined your name and didn't even offer to make it right. Hope you been thinkin' on what I offered. It's a good life, Miss Willow, and I'll be a good husband to you."

"The answer is no, Malachi Brubaker," she said stoically. "And Rafe Pierce didn't ruin my name. Nothing happened that night we were waiting out the storm. So he had no reason to make anything right. How does one make right that which has never been wrong? Good day, Baker," she said, slapping the reins on the oxen.

"You'll have a change of mind," Baker said with a big smile, and rode off toward his post at the middle of the train.

The sun was high when they stopped for half an hour at noon. The livestock enjoyed a few moments of beautiful green grass and the women took their bean patties to the edge of the river. Looking at the clean, clear running water after a week of having to put alum in muddy alkaline water just to get the sand to settle enough to boil beans in it was a blessing. Thinking about the luxury of another bath that night brought sighs and smiles to most of them.

Willow chewed the bean patties, which were no more than fried sawdust in her mouth, and washed them down with good cold water past the apple-sized lump in her throat. Aunt Harriet said once that the Lord wouldn't lead you up to nothing He wouldn't lead you through. For the first time, Willow had doubts about her great-aunt's sayings. Seemed like in the past year everything she'd been led up to hadn't worked out. First Pete, then Jake dying before she could talk to him, and now Rafe. Maybe Aunt Harriet's saying didn't take into consideration the unpredictable male.

"You going to get over him?" Gypsy asked.

"Who?" Willow raised an eyebrow.

"You know exactly who I'm talking about. Never thought he'd just ride off like that or that you'd let him. Did you have an understanding last night when you snuck off to watch your sunset or something?" Gypsy did the talking, the other three sisters did the listening.

"Didn't see him last night. Just that pesky Baker, pestering me about being his first wife. I swear I can't find a bush to squat behind without him following me." Willow tried to make a joke to get them off the subject.

"Need me to start going with you as a guard dog?" Velvet asked.

"Need someone." Willow attempted a smile but her chin quivered.

"Hey, sister, it's all right to pitch a fit." Garnet patted her arm affectionately. "We all know how you feel about that tall old drink of cold water. And we all feel bad that the old buzzard didn't return those feelings. Just remember, we're here for you. You need to talk, we'll listen. You need to be quiet, we'll understand. You need someone to kick that Baker kid into the next state, we'll line up and do the job for you."

"Thank you," Willow said, a steady stream of tears flowing down her cheeks and dripping on the collar of her shirt-waist. "I don't know whether I'm crying because of that snake in the grass, Rafe, or because I'm just realizing how much you all mean to me."

"Ah, now, hush up." Gypsy hugged her tightly. "You'll have us all and bawling like babies with the colic."

"I figure I got over the measles in ten days and they were worse than Rafe Pierce." Willow dried up the last of the tears she ever intended to shed over that man. "So I'm giving myself ten days to get over Rafe. I managed to erase

Pete from my heart in less time than that. From the time the coach left the town near his plantation in Virginia until it reached Mercersberg, Pennsylvania, I took care of the problem. I can do it now because I have done it before."

"That's the spirit," Gussie said. "Now let's finish up this day. Just nine more after this one and we'll be saying, 'Rafe who?', won't we?"

"You bet we will," Willow said, but somehow her tone didn't sound so convincing.

Day two came and went. Baker continued to remind Willow that he was available. Day three, she hardly thought of Rafe at all. Maybe only twice every hour. Her sisters helped considerably, with their good-hearted teasing about how when Willow was fifty, Baker would still be bringing in a new wife every year for her to train. Day four, Pat O'Leary kept her laughing all day, riding close to the wagon and telling her tales about his nephew, Tavish O'Leary, a short little dark-haired, blue-eyed Irishman who entertained the whole family with his gift of gab.

Day five, she awoke sobbing into her pillow. Rafe wasn't coming back. She'd thought maybe he would. He'd go home and remember their kisses and the way the whole sky lit up in a bright array of colors when their lips touched and he'd return to throw her over his shoulder and carry her off beyond the sunset to the promised land. Maybe the man at the Patee House back in St. Joe was right. There was no promised land. If there was, why would anyone believe in heaven, anyway? The day got worse as it wore on. Connie was especially hateful at every opportunity, and suddenly Willow was so weary with the trip that she didn't care anymore. She'd almost marry Baker just to be away from Connie's smart mouth and snide looks.

Day six and she was so melancholy even Patty O'Leary couldn't cheer her up. By nightfall she'd made up her mind what she was going to do. It was the only answer, really. She couldn't stand another seven months of Connie and she wasn't afraid of the challenge of doing something she'd never dreamed of before. She shut her eyes that night, not knowing what tomorrow might bring, but a deep peace finally filling her soul. Tomorrow morning she'd tell her sisters first, then Hank, and finally, Baker.

"Uncle Rafe is home," Katy's six-year-old daughter, Emily, danced around like she had hot potatoes in the toes of her boots. "Come quick, momma. It's Uncle Rafe come home."

"Well, hello, brother." Katy met him in the middle of the yard. "How'd the trip go? Have a few catfights among all those women? Most foolish wagon train trip I ever heard of Hank takin' on, but I guess the money was good. Come on in. We got a beef roast just about finished for supper, and the boys will be in from the north pasture in time to eat. They'll all be glad you're home."

"Is that bread I smell? Real yeast bread?" Rafe inhaled deeply. He was home. Home, where he'd get over the empty hole in his heart. Family would fill it all in for him, just like they'd always done.

"Of course—this is Tuesday, you know. I always bake bread on Tuesdays." Katy kept her arm around his waist as she led him into the house. Something wasn't right with Rafe. More than tiredness filled his eyes. A deep sadness. Even worse than the hollow emptiness that filled them a few years back when everything went sour with the singer.

Rafe entertained them with tales of the wagon train full of women at the supper table. He showed them the scar on his forehead and told the story of how a little lady named Willow pulled him out and sewed him up. Amid wide eyes, he related the tale of the bad men and how the same lady, Willow, rode in among them, knocking the guns from their hands and saving about fifty people from being shot dead.

Later that night, as Rafe mounted Buster to go home to his ranch, Katy leaned on the porch post and studied him. When he'd been telling the stories of the past few weeks, his eyes had glittered like they'd done before Rachel. "So her name is Willow? Why didn't you bring her with you, Rafe?" she asked.

"Because she wouldn't have come with me. Because she isn't a lady. Because she wears overalls and rides a horse astride. Because she'd fit in around here about like a cow chip in the punch bowl at a Sunday School social," Rafe said.

"Sounds kind of like weak excuses to me. Sounds like she's just the kind of woman a ranch needs. Bet if she rides astride a horse, she was probably raised up on a ranch with cattle and horses. Can do both a man's job and a woman's. Isn't too finicky to sew up a gaping hole in your head, and doesn't whine," Katy said.

"Sounds like that. Sometimes sounds like ain't reality, Katy. If she'd felt the way I do, she'd have come up those steps and spoke her mind. She can sure speak it, let me tell you, and if she'd felt even a little bit of what I felt a whole lot of, she couldn't have kept it bottled up inside," Rafe said. "I'll get over her, sister. Give me a week. By then she'll just be the lady in the funny stories."

"Okay, Rafe. It's your heart. You do what's best," Katy said.

Day one, Rafe kept so busy he figured he'd fall asleep that night and not wake until noon the next day. But memories kept appearing on the darkened ceiling of his bedroom. There was Willow, her finger poking his chest, punctuating every word when she told him she could take a wagon train all the way to Bryte, California by herself. Willow, telling the Indian children a story. Willow, in his arms, returning his kiss and not accepting his apology for it. Willow, scaling that wall down into the hollow all day long and then saving Connie's sorry, whining hide from falling. Willow, turning her back as he rode away. Was it because she couldn't bear to see him go, or was it to let him know she didn't care at all?

Day two, he awoke from barely two hours of fitful,

dream-filled sleep to face another day of hard work. His foreman, Elijah, asked him if he had a burr in his saddle all day, and if he did, would he please get it out before the next day.

"Been workin' hard while you run off to help with that trainload of howlin' women," he said, "and I don't intend for you to come home acting like this, Rafael. Worked for your Pa and raised you up on my knee, so I'm speakin' my mind. Only a woman could make a man act the way you been these past two days. So you either get that burr out of your saddle and act right or I'm going to kick you all the way back to St. Joe. Is that understood?"

"Yes, sir." Rafe grinned, but it didn't reach his eyes.

Day three, he worked twice as hard, and was careful not to be short with the hired hands. He went to bed even more miserable than he'd been in days. He fought with the visions of Willow and replaced her face with Mattie Warren's. Mattie had made no bones about her feelings toward him this past year. She flirted with him at every church social and was always at his elbow when he turned around. Her father owned the general store in Lewellen, and she was not only getting long in the tooth, at twenty-four with no husband in sight, but was also more than a little chubby. But she'd make a fine ranch wife. She'd been helping her father in the store for years, so she'd know the value of a dollar bill. He worked until daylight convincing himself that come Sunday morning he was going to begin returning Mattie's attention.

When the first sunrays filtered through the window in his bedroom, he had his hands laced behind his head, his mind made up. He knew what he had to do to finally get Willow out of his heart and mind. There was only one way and he'd simply do it. He'd tell Elijah before breakfast, Katy afterwards, and then get on his horse and ride into Lewellen.

Chapter Seventeen

W illow awoke long before daylight. Her last day on the trail, and she could hardly wait to be gone. Hank had said they could have half a day off for the wedding since they were ahead of schedule, and then Willow would ride away. Her sisters had fought with her for two days, to no avail. Her mind was made up and she was following the only thing that would make her heart stop aching.

She dressed with care, but she'd change after the wedding into her overalls and flannel shirt. She chose her best outfit, the dark blue dress she'd worn on the last leg of the journey from Mercersberg to St. Joe. Seemed only fitting that she wear the same dress to a wedding that she'd worn to a funeral. Weren't they one and the same when it was all said and done? A bride died from her own name when she took her husband's name. To her own will when she promised to obey him through good times and bad. She shook off her own negative thoughts and tried to don a smile.

"Who'd have ever thought we'd have a real wedding out here in the middle of nowhere?" Gussie took out her red satin dress and shook the wrinkles out as best she could. "And that I'd be the maid of honor. Think this dress is too short and wild?"

"I think that dress is lovely. It'll put some color in our day." Willow smiled weakly.

"Well, if you really think it's all right. I feel right dolled up when I'm wearing it," Gussie grinned. "I'm thinkin' I'll wear it if I end up having to marry one of those gold miners."

"You should. It's a pretty dress," Velvet said and meant it. Mercy, but she'd come a long way since the first time she'd wrinkled her nose at the idea of one of her own blood sisters dancing on a stage in some lowdown saloon. "I'm going to go pick a bunch of wildflowers for the bouquets. One for the bride and one for you, Gussie, and I think I've even got enough ribbon to tie a bow around them both. The bride can keep it for a keepsake that way. Who knows when she gets to her new home, what kind of hardships she might face. It might be nice to have a ribbon to remind her of her decision."

"Oh, Willow, can't we please change your mind about everything today?" Gypsy pleaded with her sister. "What you are undertaking is so dangerous, not to mention just plain foolhardy. What happens when you get there if . . ."

"You can't change my mind," Willow said. "I told you before. It's the only way I can get over this aching in my heart. I'm doing it, so just wave good-bye to me. I promise when I've settled, wherever it might be, I'll write a long letter and send it to Gussie in Bryte, California. She can read it to all of you."

"I ought to go with you," Garnet said.

"No way. You're going on to either play that piano in a saloon or find your own husband," Willow laughed. "I'll write, I promise. Soon as this wedding is finished, I'm going to ride off. No tears. Promise?"

"I ain't promising no such thing," Gypsy said. "After you're gone I'll be the baby in what's left of us Dulan sisters and babies are allowed to cry any time they want."

"You'll write to me, won't you?" Willow hugged Gypsy tightly.

"Of course, and probably blur the ink with tears. Lord, girl, you got spunk, doing what you're doing." Gypsy hugged her back.

"Not spunk. It's probably the most fool-hearted thing I've ever done." Willow managed a weak giggle around the perpetual lump in her throat. To think that she'd not even known about these four Dulan sisters until a few weeks ago and now she was hugging them good-bye, with only the hope of letters to fill in the void. But she had made up her mind and she was going to forge ahead at a full steam.

Rafe rode up to the store in Lewellen just as Mattie opened the front doors. "Need a few supplies," he said, eyeing her a bit more critically than he ever had before.

"Well, Rafael Pierce, you are home," Mattie said, pasting on her brightest smile.

"That I am, but not for long, Mattie. I need a pound of coffee, a half pound of sugar and flour, and six of those orange candy sticks in that jar." He pointed to the counter.

"That's strange," she said, filling his order and batting her eyelashes at him at the same time. "Why candy sticks? You don't have a sweet tooth. Been trying to get to your heart through your stomach for nigh onto a year now and you don't ever even taste my fine pies or cakes."

"I know, Mattie," he said. "I know, but it just wasn't meant to be. Those orange sticks remind me of the sunset, and I reckon they'll make a pretty nice present. Also, I'd like one of those plain gold wedding rings in the case there. Yes, that one. Let me hold it a minute."

She picked it out and handed it to him. "Sunsets and poetry. You know, Rafe, you like the strangest things for a man. I can't imagine wasting away time watching a silly old sunset."

He tried it on his smallest finger but it only went to the first joint. "I know, Mattie. We're just different, that's all. That's just about the right size, I think. She has small fingers."

"May I ask who's done beat my time with Lewellen's most eligible bachelor?" Mattie asked with her chin up.

"Her name is Willow Gail Dulan and I don't even know if she'll have me, but I intend to go prepared. I shouldn't have left the wagon train without speaking up, but I did. So now after three days, I've got to backtrack and hope she's of the same mind I am," Rafe said.

"Well, if she ain't, you can always trade that ring in for a bigger one." Mattie wiggled her fingers at him. "And if she is, then bring her around. No hard feelings and she might need a friend, Rafe."

"Thanks, Mattie. You are a jewel," Rafe said.

"Yeah, well, if you ain't going to take this jewel home to your ranch, then I've a mind to flirt a bit with your sister's brother-in-law," Mattie said. "Just didn't want to start up nothing if there was a chance with you."

"John?" Rafe asked skeptically.

"Sure," Mattie said. "He's been making an extra trip or two to town at night to buy things he don't need. I think he's about to ask me out to the Sunday picnic after church."

"Well, we'll be right glad to have you in the family, I'm sure. And if Willow comes back to Lewellen with me, I'll introduce you to her first thing," Rafe laughed. So John was interested in Mattie. Now that was a match made in heaven. John loved sweet food so much that he had an extra roll of fat just above his belt. The Lord, Himself couldn't have put two better people together.

He filled his saddlebags with supplies and rode out at a steady pace toward Ash Hollow. They had a three-day jump on him, but he figured in just three more days he could catch them by doubling the amount of miles they'd be able for each day. Six days separation from Willow was almost more than he could bear the thought of, but three of them were behind him. With any luck, in a week to ten days they'd be back at the ranch. He looked up at the cloudless blue sky and sent up a prayer, begging the Almighty to please let Willow love him.

* * *

Willow helped Gussie fix her hair up on top of her head in an array of curls and then helped Velvet tie the ribbons around the bouquets. The other women in the wagon train had prepared a cake of sorts. It wasn't the fancy cake Willow would have had at her wedding festivities with Pete. That particular cake was supposed to have been the envy of every new bride in all of Pennsylvania. But the ladies had done their best with the limited supplies they'd had to work with, so the bride would appreciate their efforts.

Everyone gathered in rows, exactly as if they were in a church building rather than outside under the morning sun. The only difference was that they were standing rather than sitting on church pews. Hank and the groom took their places under the shade of a big ash tree, and Garnet played the wedding march on a guitar the groom had hidden away.

Gussie appeared from behind a wagon and walked slowly down the aisle. Her red satin dress picked up the sunbeams and glistened. Wildflowers of bright red, orange, yellow, pink, and white, were wrapped up in a flowing white ribbon and were also arranged in the curls on top of her head.

When Gussie reached the front of the gathering, the bride appeared at the back of the pretend church. Her blond hair was arranged like Gussie's, but she'd opted for only orange and yellow flowers in her hair. The blue skirt and shirtwaist formed over her petite figure, showing off a tiny waist and an ample bosom. She carried a bouquet like Gussie's, only slightly bigger with longer ribbons. She didn't seem to notice that Gussie's dress was mid-calf or that the petticoats underneath were black lace and hung about an inch below the hem of the dress. She just kept her eyes firmly fixed on the groom's blue ones as she made her way down the aisle and hoped she'd made the right decision.

"Dearly beloved, we are gathered here this fine morning to join these two young people in holy matrimony." Hank raised his voice. "I don't often get to use my authority in this capacity, but this morning I'm glad to be of service to these two folks, who have assured me they are truly in love and will do all they can to make their marriage last. Even though they come from two very different backgrounds, the groom has declared that he will stay true to one wife for the rest of his life. Elsewise, I couldn't perform this ceremony. Now let us begin. If there is anyone here who has a reason why this couple should not be married, let them speak now or forever hold their peace."

Rafe rode into the camp and saw the gathering on top of the hill. The women were wearing their finery and the first thing he saw was Gussie Dulan stepping out from behind a wagon. She wore a red satin dancing dress and carried a bouquet of flowers and strolled down the . . . aisle? His mind kicked into overtime. There was a wedding going on. And there was Willow standing with her back to him in front of Hank. She had the other bouquet of flowers. Holy smoke. That wimpy little Brubaker kid had talked her into marrying him after all—and Rafe was too late.

He heard Hank begin the ceremony and then say something about the man promising in spite of his background to keep true to one wife. Every thought in Rafe's brain told him to ride away from it all. Willow didn't love him or she wouldn't have consented to marry that kid. And just six days after he'd left.

But his heart said he'd rode hard for three days and he was going to speak his mind. Even if it made a complete fool out of him in front of his old friend Hank and all the women on the train. He'd planned a much more private visit with Willow, but if it had to be in front of a hundred witnesses, so be it.

He kneed Buster in the ribs and made it to the back of the group just as Hank asked if there were any present who had objections to the marriage. "I do," he yelled as he rode the horse right down the center of the aisle.

"I have objections. I want thirty minutes with this bride alone, and then if she wants to marry this pipsqueak, I'll ride out," he said, riding right up behind Willow.

Amusement glittered in Hank's eyes. So the prodigal lover had come back to lay claim to a bride. "Rafe, I'll talk to you after the ceremony," Hank whispered.

"Look, Momma Annie, Uncle Rafe has come back. But why does he want to marry that woman?" Rafe heard Merry whisper loudly behind him.

"Who is this man?" The groom looked at his bride.

"I have no idea. I've never seen him before," she whispered, her voice on the verge of tears.

"Well, he evidently knows you, to want thirty minutes of private time," the groom hissed.

"I think we'd better postpone this wedding for thirty minutes," Hank chuckled. "I want you two to come with me, and sit under this shade tree," he said to the bride and groom. "Rafe, I want you to turn around. I think the blond-haired woman you are looking for is standing way back there in the congregation. This bride right here is Melody Parsons and her intended is Richard Olson. They happen to be running away from Utah and going to Nebraska to live with Melody's parents until they can get a homestead of their own. Seems he's forsaking his religion for her and she's forsaking an aunt she was living with in Utah."

"Oh." Rafe looked at the bride and realized then that she wasn't Willow. Same height. Same build, almost. This woman had a little more in the bosom area, but the same blond curly hair. Melody's eyes were a rich dark brown and the groom, bless his heart, was almost as white as pure snow. If it hadn't been so confusing, Rafe might have found it funny.

"You looking for me?" Willow said at his side. "If you are, then you better get off that horse 'cause I don't intend to stand here looking up into the hot sun at you while you talk."

Gussie began to laugh and it infected the whole crowd. Some of them giggled so hard they got the hiccups while others merely wiped their eyes with hankies they had hidden away in their sleeves.

"I reckon I can do that," Rafe said amid the laughter. "Think we might take a walk up there on that hill? I've rode a long way to talk to you."

"I reckon we might." Willow walked slowly beside him until they were out of hearing distance of the rest of the congregation. She sat down on the grass.

Rafe did the same, being very careful not to touch her. One touch and he'd be a begging, whimpering fool. "I got home and tried to forget all about what we shared, Willow. I worked hard for three days and tried to think of another woman there in Lewellen who'd make me a good wife. It didn't work."

"I know." She placed her small hand over his and tingles played chase up and down his spine. "Yesterday, these two kids came riding up to the front of our wagon train and asked Hank if he'd marry them. They'd been on the trail a week or more and her reputation was already ruined. He figured his parents had disowned him since he was leaving that faith like Baker has. So Hank said he'd do the job this morning and we could have a morning off for the festivities. I worried all night trying to make the right decision, but when I did, it brought peace to my heart. When the wedding was finished, I was going to get on that saddled horse back there at our wagon, soon as I changed into my overalls, and I was riding to Lewellen to tell you just how I feel."

"You were? Good Lord, Willow, if that ain't the dumbest thing you've done yet! Don't you know there's highway pirates out there, not to mention hostile Indians? You might've been killed!" He jerked his hand free from hers and jumped to his feet, pointing his finger like a gun with the trigger already pulled back.

"Looks like they're getting along just fine," Gussie told her sisters from the vantage point she kept at the front of the congregation. "He's yelling and I swear I can see sparks flying between them, not to mention the ones shooting out of her Dulan blue eyes."

"Betcha we got a double wedding in half an hour," Gypsy said.

"I ain't losin' my money." Garnet laughed.

"Now we don't have to worry about her out there all alone on the trails," Velvet said.

"Hmmph." Gypsy snorted. "Worry about her? We shoulda been worryin' about the men who would try to take advantage of her."

"Don't you yell at me!" Willow screamed back at Rafe, loud enough that the sisters could hear her plain as if she was standing right next to them. She'd gotten to her feet and her nose was so close to his they made a single silhouette against the bright sun.

What am I to do? Rafe wondered. Finally an answer came floating across the plains. *Forget words. Forget arguing.* The way to tame Willow wasn't with words but actions. He reached forward, wrapped his arms around her waist, and pulled her to his chest. By the time she realized what he was doing, he already had his mouth on hers and the kiss went on and on. Willow wished it would never end.

"Now," he said breathlessly when he released her, "I've come to ask you to marry me, Willow. I guess since the church is already full and there's a bridesmaid up there in front of the ladies, we could take care of it right here and now?"

"And then what?" she asked, just as breathless.

"Then we'll ride out of here. You can get on that horse and I'll get on Buster and we'll go see what lies beyond those sunsets we both enjoy so much. I got a ring." He pulled the gold band from his pocket.

"Pretty sure of yourself, weren't you?" She took it from his hand and tried it on. It fit perfectly, and even though it wasn't the big diamond Pete had given her, it was even more beautiful as the sun sparkled on the gold.

"Just hoping." He drew her back for another kiss.

"Hey, you ain't supposed to be kissing the bride until after the ceremony," the groom called from the bottom of the hill.

"Yes, Rafe, yes, I will marry you this day. But only if I can wear my overalls on the trip back to Lewellen," she said.

"Honey, you can wear anything or nothing. I'll just be happy to ride along beside you for the rest of my life," he said, breathing in the freshness of her freshly washed blond hair.

"I'll keep you to those words. About riding along with me for our whole lives, Rafe. I won't have another woman causing problems in our world." She looked up at him seriously.

"Honey, I reckon you can cause enough problems in our world all by yourself," he said.

"And don't you forget it!" She took him by the hand and led him back down the hill. "We're having a double wedding. Hank, let's get this show on the road. I intend to be a third of the way to Lewellen, Nebraska by the time the sun sets tonight."

"Yes, ma'am," Hank laughed. He'd just get another one of those marriage forms from the supply wagon and put them in the registry at the next town they came to. "I reckon we can dispense with the opening remarks and the part about someone disagreeing with these two couples getting married. Let's get right to the vows. You stand here, Richard and Rafe. You ladies stand here. Gussie, you stop shedding tears or I'm sending you back there with the rest of the weeping Dulan sisters. Mercy, wasn't a one of you cried like this at your Pa's funeral, even."

"Hush and preach," Gussie said.

Hank did the shortest ceremony in his entire profession of marrying folks. "And now you two grooms may kiss the brides. But wait a minute," Hank grinned. "Rafael, you have to kiss this woman and Richard, you kiss this one. I don't want you to get confused again, Rafe."

Willow melted into his arms. His at last. They might have a rocky road some times but she'd be there beside him all the way to the end, he had no doubt. He raised her chin and kissed her, making the sassy Willow Gail Dulan his wife.

Later that night, they sat beside a river and watched a gorgeous orange sunset. Rafe produced a candy stick from his saddle bags and told her that he'd thought of her and their sunsets when he'd seen the jar at the Lewellen General Store. She leaned into his embrace and kissed him again. What a wonderful wedding gift. A simple candy stick, and the promise of living a lifetime together in the promised land out there beyond the sunset.

9/04

DISCARDED